Black Friday: Exposed

Black Friday: Exposed

Ashley & JaQuavis

www.urbanbooks.net

Urban Books, LLC
78 East Industry Court
Deer Park, NY 11729

ISBN 13: 978-1-60162-445-1
ISBN 10: 1-60162-445-X

First Mass Market Printing April 2011
First Trade Paperback Printing April 2010
Printed in the United States of America

10 9 8 7 6 5 4 3 2 1

Distributed by Kensington Publishing Corp.
Submit Wholesale Orders to:
Kensington Publishing Corp.
C/O Penguin Group (USA) Inc.
Attention: Order Processing
405 Murray Hill Parkway
East Rutherford, NJ 07073-2316
Phone: 1-800-526-0275
Fax: 1-800-227-9604

Prologue

Kasheef's heart felt as if it would explode as he sat in the federal courtroom. News cameras were littered throughout; while both supporters and the opposition awaited the verdict. It was the day that he would meet his fate, the day that the rest of his days would be determined by the decision that the jury rendered. On the outside Kasheef was calm and collected. His chocolate Armani suit rested perfectly against his dark skin and medium athletic build. With his hair cut neatly in a fresh ceaser and his eyes filled with sincerity, one would never guess that the man sitting before them was a drug kingpin. A distinguished business man yes, but a drug kingpin no. Kasheef scanned the jury with his eyes and couldn't read their expressions. He didn't know what tomorrow held for him and for the first time in his life he was afraid. Prison was not an option for him. To lock him up would be equivalent to stealing his pride and he refused to live on his knees. Being told when to eat, sleep, how frequently he could use the phone, and monitoring who he interacted with; was not an appealing lifestyle for him. The harsh reality of being locked up was not for him. The life and times of an inmate wasn't for him. Kasheef hoped and prayed that the verdict would be delivered in his favor, because if it wasn't he was already prepared to go out in a blaze of glory. A $10,000 cash payment to one of the assigned court officers ensured that he would have his weapon of choice, a chrome .45, taped underneath the defense table. He discreetly ran his hand along the underside of the cherry wood and felt the cold steel that was strapped securely in place. It was his insurance policy.

Kasheef was not green to the game and had been in the dope game since he was a young boy so he knew that his day of judgment was inevitable. While many glamorized the street life, he knew the real deal and was well aware that his reign could only end in one of two ways—prison or death. He would much rather hold court in the streets for his actions, in his own environment, where he would at least have a chance to survive. Sitting in a courtroom made him a sitting duck. He knew that it was very possible that the jury would convict him and that the judge would throw the book at him, sending him away for the remainder of his natural life. He turned and stared into the eyes of Norelle, his girlfriend, who greeted him with a wink and a sexy smirk. Cameras flashed continuously in her face, but she took it all in stride. She knew that they had recognized her face from her very public arrest that had occurred the day before. Almost as soon as she was handcuffed, she was released. Bail money was not an issue and now she sat silently with her fingers crossed as she awaited Kasheef's verdict. Norelle's own legal troubles were non-existent at the moment. The only thing that mattered to her was what was going on right now. Kasheef had to admit that Norelle was a beautiful girl. From her Manolo stilettos, to her Marc Jacobs two-piece suit with the matching clutch; she represented all that he was. From rags to riches, he had taken her from the gutter and put her in a throne beside his own as the queen of the streets. She held her title well and, indeed like royalty, commanded attention. *You didn't think I would come,* she mouthed.

"All rise!" the bailiff announced loudly, causing Kasheef to turn back around in his chair. "The Honorable Judge Campbell Martin presiding."

"Be seated," the judge mumbled as he took his own behind the large pedestal. "Has the jury reached a decision?"

The face of the foreman told Kasheef all that he needed to know. Kasheef gripped the steel underneath the table and took a deep breath as he prepared himself for what was about to go down.

"Yes we have, your Honor."

"And what say you?" the judge inquired.

"We the jury . . ."

Kasheef's hand wrapped tightly around the gun.

"Find the defendant . . ."

His heartbeat in his ears, blocked out all sound as he watched the foreman's lips mouth the words.

Pow! Pow! Pow!

The verdict fell on deaf ears as the courtroom erupted in mayhem . . .

Chapter One

(Six Months Earlier)

Norelle looked at the clock and the more time that passed, the more irritated she became. It was already one in the morning and Kasheef still hadn't come home. She folded the clothes that she had spread out on her bed and packed them neatly inside her Louis Vuitton tote. *This nigga knows we've got to catch a plane tomorrow morning. He should've been back. He's so unreliable. All I need is one weekend. One weekend when it is just about me. He can't even give me that,* she thought to herself. She was anxious for her sorority reunion. It had been six years since she'd seen any of her sorority sisters and when she'd gotten the invitation to go on a reunion cruise with them she was ecstatic. She knew that everyone would be there, along with their significant others, so she made sure she told Kasheef way in advance so that he could put her on his schedule. Having a man as fine as Kasheef was a plus. His dark, prominent features, sleepy bedroom eyes, and amazing physique were every woman's fantasy. He was even taller than she was, which was definitely a perk. Usually, most men who had been blessed with his type of features had also been cursed financially. Fine men were always the maintenance men, or the construction workers you admired in passing. Kasheef, however, was the total package. He had pockets as deep as the Pacific Ocean, and he was willing to fulfill all of her material desires. This in itself gave her bragging rights. His looks and charm, along with the many diamonds he had blessed her with was sure to make her the envy of all of her old friends. Not to mention the semi-successful modeling career she had. There was one person in particular that she was excited about running into; her best friend Carmen. They were close and Carmen had been like a sister to her during their time at Spelman. Like so many others, they had promised to never lose touch after graduation, but life interjected, and intimate conversations everyday became occasional courtesy calls. She couldn't wait to see her and she couldn't wait for Carmen to meet Kasheef. He wasn't perfect, but he was hers and Norelle couldn't wait to show him off. *If the nigga make it,* she thought angrily as she watched the clock strike 1:30. *He's not even packed yet.* Carmen pulled his luggage out of the closet and tossed it onto the bed as she threw his drawers and socks inside. She was trying to give Kasheef the benefit of the doubt, but once 2:00 A.M. found her bed still empty she couldn't help but pick up the phone. *He better answer my call.*

"Why'd you want to meet up here in Queens? We always do business at your spot in Long Island," Ahmad slurred as he stared around the crowded night club and shifted uncomfortably in his seat. The atmosphere was loud and boisterous. It was definitely not the environment to be talking money. The club was popping as young men and women entered, dressed in their best attire.

Kasheef looked at the man in front of him, studying him intensely for a few seconds before he replied, "I felt like switching things up. This is my club. Wires can't pick up a signal in here."

"What you think I'm wired up fam?"

"I don't know *fam* . . . are you?" Kasheef responded as he stared Ahmad directly in the eyes, trying to sense any form of deception. He was not the type to play games or beat around the bush. If he had suspicions about a person he put them on the table. It was important for him to have thorough people around him. Real men respected his bluntness, because they knew the game and followed the same rules that he did.

"Yo', Sheef you ill'n right now son. I've been copping my weight from you for years fam, don't insult me," Ahmad stated seriously.

Kasheef had done business with Ahmad for the past two years and they had never encountered any problems. Ahmad always had his money on time and it was always on point. He knew that he was wrong for doubting his man, but Kasheef would rather be safe than sorry. In this game there wasn't any room for error. Ahmad had caught a little one year bid behind an illegal gun charge; and Kasheef thought that it was a bit odd that, upon his release, Ahmad was back in the streets full force, attempting to cop his normal order of forty bricks. Kasheef would have preferred for Ahmad to be more cautious and lay low for a couple months before delving back into the game, but he was a grown man and Kasheef wasn't into schooling niggas. He kept to himself so that his name would never pop out on federal radar. He had to make sure Ahmad had not switched sides.

"You're right fam, I'm on some other shit. You know with all these niggas bumping they gums like bitches you can't be too careful," Kasheef said hesitantly as he relaxed some and leaned back in the booth with his shot glass extended in the air.

"No doubt," Ahmad responded with a half smile. He raised his glass as well and tapped it against Kasheef's. "Now that you got your panties out of a bunch—about this business—"

The ringing of the Kasheef's phone stopped Ahmad in midsentence as he looked at the caller ID, noticing it was Norelle. He put up his finger to signal for Ahmad to put his conversation on hold and then picked up the call. "What's good?"

"You tell me Sheef. I thought you would be home by now," Norelle stated. She tried to keep her tone in check because she knew that Kasheef did not appreciate disrespect, but even in her best attempt her attitude was apparent. *This nigga want a whole lot of respect for somebody who keeps playing me to the left. When he starts keeping respectful hours maybe I'll hold my tongue a little bit more,* she thought angrily.

"I'm handling this business right now. I'll be there," he replied vaguely.

"Babe, you know we have to catch a plane tomorrow. You're not even packed." Her voice went from angry to desperate. Norelle was high maintenance and a very dependent woman. She hated to be kept waiting. It made her feel unimportant.

"Yeah, I said I'll be there. Give me a minute," he stated in a disengaged tone.

Kasheef smirked as he watched Ahmad pull the arm of a young woman passing by their table. He peeped her from head to toe and licked his lips as his eyes focused on her apple shaped behind.

"Sheef?" Norelle whined into the phone, knowing he wasn't paying attention to her.

"I'm here," he answered in irritation and focused his attention back on his call.

"Where are you anyway? You in the club?" she asked heatedly.

Unwilling to hear her bitching, he ended the call quickly. "Don't wait up ma. I'll be there after I handle this business. Don't worry about your reunion. I'll be packed and ready by the time you wake up." Before she could protest, he put the dial tone to her ear and closed his cell.

Ahmad was kicking game to his company so Kasheef decided to lay low and let his man enjoy his freedom. He called one of the waitresses over and ordered a round of drinks.

"What you drinking on ma?" Kasheef asked the girl that Ahmad was with.

"Call me Alija," she said with a dazzling smile. Her golden soft MAC lip gloss glistened and her perfectly straight teeth were enticing to Kasheef.

The fact that she looked him directly in the eye was a turn on for him. She wasn't shy and had the confidence of a supermodel.

"Okay Alija, what you drinking?" he repeated as he returned her stare. He had to admit the girl was gorgeous. Her almond colored skin and jet black hair complimented her chinky hazel eyes. Her body was flawless in the Juicy Couture she was rocking. She was dressed casually, yet he still found her sexy. She did not have to show it all in order to catch his eye. He was attracted and curious as to the hidden treasure that lied beneath the expensive fabric of her clothes. He had to remind himself of the real woman he had at home in Norelle, just to break her stare. He allowed Ahmad to chill out and kept the drinks coming all night to show his boy a good homecoming. He made sure that he didn't get to tipsy, remembering the business that was still left unattended. The night came to a close around four in the morning as the party goers began to vacate the club.

"It was nice to meet you both. I had a good time," Alija said as she stood up from the table. "Call me," she said to Ahmad. She gave him a sexy wink before she left and Kasheef could not stop his eyes from following her backside as she sashayed away from the table.

Kasheef and Ahmad waited until the club cleared out before they ascended the steps to the loft office above. "I see you doing you again," Kasheef stated as he sat down in his leather office chair.

Ahmad laughed drunkenly and wobbled a little bit as he approached a chair.

"You good baby?" Kasheef asked, noticing Ahmad's lack of balance.

"I'm a'ight baby boy. I'm good . . . trying to get this money nah mean?" Ahmad replied, a little too loudly.

Kasheef felt his phone vibrate and he picked it up, noticing Norelle's name on the ID. He sent her to voicemail and sighed. The fact that she wasn't asleep let him know that she was up just waiting for him to walk through the door. He knew that there would be hell to pay when he arrived home. The longer he stayed out, the higher Norelle's temperature would rise. When he finally did step foot inside their door, she would be ready to blow. He shook his head in regret because he knew that he was only adding fuel to the fire by ignoring her call. He needed to wrap up his business so that he could hurry to the crib. He didn't want beef with Norelle because he knew that it would take a couple shopping sprees to make her happy again. It was in his best interest to wrap up the night. It would save him a couple thousand dollars in the end.

Alija walked through the crowd in the parking lot as she made her way to her car. Her girls had all found men to kick it with after the club, but she was exhausted and also had a child to go home to. She switched her way to the car and stopped midway once she realized she'd forgotten her clutch purse. She'd set it down when she was entertaining Ahmad and Kasheef. "Damn it!" she yelled as she took off her stiletto pumps and held them in her hand as she went back into the club. It was completely empty when she stepped inside so she quickly made her way back to the table. "Okay, where is my purse?" she mumbled tiredly. "Damn it!" Noticing that a light was shining from the second level, she made her way upstairs to see who was still in the club. She hoped that there was a manager still working so that she could see if someone had turned in her belongings. Unaware of what she was stepping into, she peeked her head around the corner and into the room.

"So how many you need?" Kasheef asked Ahmad as he walked to his wall safe and began to put in the combination.

Ahmad stood up on wobbly legs. "Yo', fam it was jumping in this mu'fucka tonight," he said in slurred speech. As he spoke he stepped closer to Kasheef. Kasheef noticed his man was wild'n. Ahmad had never been the boisterous, show boating type, but tonight he was in rare form. He dismissed Ahmad's unusual behavior. He knew that Ahmad had been locked up for a year. If you added that with the fact that he was a little twisted from the nonstop flow of liquor it was understandable how Ahmad could be acting out of his usual calm demeanor.

Kasheef laughed lightly and opened the safe. "I hear you fam. How many you want though? Let's finish this so I can break out." When he turned around he was staring down the barrel of a 9 mm.

"All of em'! Clear that mu'fuckin' safe out nigga!" Ahmad yelled perfectly coherent, as he pressed the pistol to Kasheef's dome at point blank range.

Kasheef's blood boiled as he ice grilled the man before him. He instantly regretted that he hadn't followed his first mind. "I see you sobered up," he remarked with venom.

"I see you slipping fam. Don't take this personally though baby. It's all in the game nigga, so just be easy and empty out that safe."

Kasheef nodded his head and reached into the safe and began removing bricks of heroine slowly, one by one. "You had to do it like this fam?" Kasheef said without emotion, vying for time as he frantically put the clip in the unloaded gun inside his safe. He knew that it was almost impossible to do with one hand and when Ahmad clocked him upside his temple with his weapon, he knew that he was close to death.

"You think I'm stupid fam?" Ahmad yelled as he cocked his gun and fired a warning shot into the air. "Let me see them hands!"

Kasheef heard someone gasp at the door and when Ahmad averted his eyes Kasheef took his shot. In one swift motion he reached inside the safe, loaded his pistol, and blasted off without hesitation.

Boom!

The blast from the gun resounded loudly throughout the building, bouncing from wall to wall until it met with Alija's ears. Shocked and in terror her eyes grew big as she silently regretted witnessing something that she was never meant to see. Her eyes met Kasheef's. She stared at him, he stared at her; in distress, they both waited to gauge the other's reaction.

Run Alija! Move before this nigga kills you too!

When the words finally registered in her brain, Alija took off. Instinctively, she quickly stepped out of her shoes and with them in hand she descended the steps two at a time. The gunshot had been so loud that it felt like bells were going off in her ears. "Oh shit . . . oh shit," she whispered as she felt herself becoming nauseous. Vomit tickled the back of her throat as she tried her hardest to hold it down before it erupted.

"Yo'!" Kasheef yelled after her as he ran up on her and grabbed her elbow. She fought him viciously, slapping and kicking for her life.

"No! Let me go! You killed him!" she gasped as she tried her hardest to free herself from his hold. "Please . . . please I won't tell. I swear to God!" Their struggle ensued, but when Alija finally snatched her arm away from him she lost her bearings and the long fall down the remainder of the stairs introduced her face to the hard cement floor. She felt the pain that echoed throughout her limbs, but she couldn't afford to let it slow her down. Frantically, she attempted to stand. Before she could get off of the ground, Kasheef had descended the steps and blocked her path to safety.

"Calm the fuck down!" he growled menacingly as he grabbed her by both shoulders and shook her until she was quiet.

"Oh my God. You killed him," she whispered as she doubled over crying. She was unable to silence herself, but afraid of the retributions for making so much noise.

"Listen," he said through closed teeth as he grabbed her chin. His gaze penetrated through her and she could see her impending death in his eyes. "You ain't see shit, you don't know shit; nah mean?"

She nodded her head up and down. With her fear controlling her reflexes she shook violently as she cried uncontrollably. She was unable to stop the sobs that were spilling out of her, but she tried desperately; afraid that if she did not be quiet than Kasheef would surely murder her where she stood.

"Go home . . . and keep your fucking mouth shut, you heard?"

She raised her shaking hands in front of her defensively and replied, "Thank you. I swear I won't say anything."

Kasheef watched her walk out of the club. He knew that he had broken the number one rule and that was to never ever leave any witnesses, but something had held him back from taking the young girl's life. He did not like the fear that he could cause another person to have. The look of terror on the girl's face frightened even Kasheef. He was afraid of the amount of power he held. He felt inhumane and sometimes resented the cruelty and suffering he had inflicted in the streets. He watched as Alija sped off recklessly from the scene and then placed a call to some of his goons. He needed to get the body out of his office and he needed to do it quick.

Alija rushed into her two bedroom apartment and made sure she locked the dead bolt behind her. "Oh my God! What just happened . . . what in the fuck just happened," she repeated over and over again as she paced back and forth over the hardwood floor. "How did I get myself into this?" she asked herself as tears fell from her eyes. She could not get the scene out of her head. The blood—so much blood, and the deafening blast of the gunshot resonated in her ears. Each time she closed her eyes all she saw was the red flow of blood as it left from Ahmad's body. She felt like she could not breathe and her hands felt dirty. She snatched her shirt off of her body and rubbed her bare skin to calm the rising goose bumps on her skin. She ran into the bathroom, kicking off the rest of her clothes on the way, and jumped into the shower—not even waiting for the water to heat up. She scrubbed her skin roughly, as if she could cleanse her soul of the sin she'd just witnessed. She had never seen a dead body before and there was a guilty pit in her stomach as if she had committed the crime herself. She sat down in the basin of the bathtub and wrapped her arms around her knees as the water cascaded from the shower head above; tears mixed with water as she cried her fear away.

Knock! Knock!

"Alija is everything okay in there?" she heard her sister Mickie yell through the bathroom door.

Alija stood up and rinsed her body before stepping out of the shower. "Yeah girl, everything's fine. I'll be out in a minute." Her voice cracked as she spoke as she tried to compose her rattled nerves. She dried her body, slipped into her silk pajamas, and walked into her room. Her sister and her six month old daughter lay together peacefully. Alija lifted the covers and lay on the empty side of the bed as she kissed her baby girl gently on the cheek.

"You sure everything's okay?" Mickey asked as she sat up and gazed worriedly at her sister.

"Yeah Mick, I'm good," she answered despondently as she closed her eyes.

Red filled the space between her eyelids and she quickly opened them back up.

"Oh yeah, your baby daddy called," Mickey stated.

Alija didn't reply.

"Alija did you hear me?" she asked.

"Yeah I hear you. I'm just tired. Get some sleep Mick. Thanks for watching Nahla for me."

With those words, Mickey went back to sleep and Alija tried to figure out how she would ever rest again with such a heavy burden weighing down her heart.

Norelle was at home—heated. She was beyond the point of sleep. She was in full blown bitch mode and didn't care what excuse Kasheef came home with. It was going down as soon as he walked through the door. There was no stopping the neglect, jealousy, and rage she felt at that moment. She wasn't even going to try to keep her composure. World War III was in the making because the two of them were about to clash; egos and all. She heard his keys jingle in the lock and before he could even step foot inside she asked, "See how you do me? Do you see the shit you take me through?"

He stepped into her view and when she saw all the blood on his shirt her attitude went out of the window. "Oh my God! Are you hurt?" she asked frantically as she rushed to his side. The innate concern of a woman for her man kicked in and her heart instantly worried for the safety of Kasheef.

"I'm good," he stated as he gently pushed her aside.

"Kasheef what happened tonight?" she asked as she frowned at the obvious brush off. He sat down and put his face in his hands as he attempted to gather his thoughts.

"Listen. If anybody ever asks you . . . and I'm not saying they will, but if it ever does come up . . . I was here with you all night," Kasheef instructed.

"Tell me what happened Kasheef. Where did all of this blood come from? Oh my God Kasheef what is going on? You're covered in blood!" she yelled, her voice pinched in fright as she stared at Kasheef with a worried gaze; waiting for an answer.

"Norelle, stop asking all these fucking questions! Just do what I say a'ight? You're down for your man right?"

"Yeah you know that," she whispered, her eyes searching his as she attempted to prove that she could be the type of woman he could trust with his life; his ride or die chick.

"Then make sure you tell anybody who comes asking that I was here all night."

"Okay," she agreed without hesitation.

Kasheef stood up and kissed her on the forehead. "Go get some sleep. We'll leave first thing tomorrow for this reunion. It looks like your little trip came right on time." She nodded her head and retired to their bedroom as her mind wandered into the night.

Chapter Two

"Okay. My bags are packed, all of my clients have been informed of my trip, all of my legal documents have been sent over to the courthouse, and . . ." Carmen sat at her desk and thumbed through her planner as she tried to jog her memory. "What am I forgetting Dawn?" she asked her secretary who was standing before her with a legal pad and pen in hand.

"Did you pack your needle and thread? You know what salt water can do to a sew in," the petite white girl replied as she looked at Carmen's hair skeptically with a playful smile on her face. She knew that her boss hated to get her weave wet and could not help but to slip in a joke before she left.

"My weave is just fine, fuck you very much," Carmen replied with a smile. "I get my wig done at the best salon in New York so that's not an issue. Now what else?" Carmen and Dawn were the only young female employees at the prestigious white law firm. Most of the other women were at least twenty years older than Carmen and Dawn, so the pair naturally had more in common because they were both in their late twenties. They had worked with each other for over five years so they were very comfortable with one another. Carmen didn't want to be the type of boss who rode a high horse. She was pleasant and friendly. She loved to have a good time, but when she was working with a client, or concentrating on a case; it was all business. She took her job very seriously. Graduating top of her class at Spelman and then on to Howard Law for graduate school made her the cream of the crop amongst African American attorneys. Affirmative action got her through the door at one of the most reputable firms on the East Coast, but once she was there she found that she had to prove herself to her chauvinistic predominantly white co-workers. They always gave her the bottom of the barrel cases and she defended low profile criminals. She had to work ten times harder and so far she had done a damned good job by never losing a case. Dawn respected her as a person, went with the flow of the ever changing work environment, and understood Carmen's desire to excel so they vibed easily.

"Let's see," Dawn said thinking aloud. "Did you pack your condoms? God knows how long it's been since you've had some and who knows you may get lucky. Maybe you'll find one of those sexy island men with twelve inches and a smile like Taye Diggs."

Carmen scowled while shaking her head and replied, "You know what? You are not helping right now. Just make sure you keep everything in order here. The last thing I need is to come back from this trip and have a million and one messes to clean up."

"Yes ma'am. Now will you get out of here and have fun," Dawn said practically pushing Carmen out of her office.

Carmen grabbed her briefcase and headed out the door. She hopped into her Mercedes CLK and sped off toward the airport. She couldn't wait to unwind and have a good time with her old college sisters.

Things between Norelle and Kasheef were un-usually awkward. An uncomfortable silence filled the space between them and they purposefully avoided each other as they prepared for their trip. Norelle didn't know exactly what had gone down the night before, but she was positive that it was something serious. All of the blood had been proof that Kasheef had been involved in something illegal. The fact that Kasheef was distant and solemn let her know that he was worried about whatever had gone down. She felt like she was walking around on eggshells as she moved around their home and she silently began to question whether Kasheef could provide the type of life she wanted. She had enjoyed the fruits of his street labor by being his woman. She was known city wide in every borough just off of the strength that she was Kasheef's girl. Being amongst the hood's elite was one of the perks of being involved with a hood fella, but the negative side of the game was beginning to rear its ugly head, and she was not so sure that she could live up to the expectations of being a hustler's wife. She was expected to hold her man down in his weakest and lowest point, but knew that she would not be the one to stand tall. She did not know exactly what had gone down the night before and it was obvious Kasheef did not want to divulge the information to her, but she felt it in her bones that whatever it was, was about to change the direction of her life. She knew her man and Kasheef was worried. Norelle had never seen him like this. She only hoped and prayed that he would be able to keep up the extravagant lifestyle that she had become accustomed to. The money is what made her loyal to Kasheef and if that ever disappeared, she hated to admit it, but there was a great possibility that she would too. It sounded cruel, but she was a practical woman and her motto was: *What's Love Got to Do With It?*

"Are you almost ready?" Kasheef asked dryly as he put on a fitted Yankees cap.

"Yeah I'm good . . ." she replied as she grabbed her tote. She looked up at Kasheef. "Is everything okay?"

"It's nothing for you to worry about. I'll get your bags, you grab the keys to the car," he instructed.

The car ride to the airport was quiet and the silence was deafening. After twenty minutes of driving, Norelle finally turned to Kasheef and said, "Listen you don't have to go if you don't—"

"I'm going," he said cutting her off. "I need to get out of the city for a couple days anyway. Let things cool down. I'll get some sleep on the plane and be in a better mood a'ight?"

She nodded her head skeptically.

"Don't worry about it. This is your weekend. Just have a good time," he finished as he kissed her forehead.

Kasheef and Norelle walked up to the port and were amazed at the size of the ship. Nei-

ther of them had been on a cruise before and
was pleasantly surprised when they pulled up.
Norelle was like a kid in a candy store and the
smile that graced her face lightened the mood
for Kasheef. He had never seen her this excited
and the warm Miami sun seemed to melt his cold
exterior away. They checked their bags and then
checked in before boarding the ship. Every single
passenger on the boat was forced to attend the
safety precaution meeting, so Norelle took the
opportunity to look for anyone she knew. The
sorority wasn't the only patrons on the massive
ship so Norelle had a hard time finding any of
her sorors. She figured that she would see them
all at the welcome dinner that evening so she
didn't stress it too much. "Look at this shit," Kasheef stated in amazement as they stepped into
the main atrium which allowed them to see each
level of the ship.

"I know it's crazy. I didn't expect everything
to be this grand I guess," Norelle replied. Norelle
found that their ocean view suite and the size of
it reminded her of a very small studio apartment
in New York.

"As much bread as I broke for this room it's
kind of small," Kasheef commented as he slid
the balcony door open and stepped out into the
fresh air.

"It's a ship boy, it can't be too big," Norelle laughed as she joined him. He wrapped his arms around her waist and leaned in toward her. His hard body felt good against her and she parted her lips to meet his tongue with a passionate kiss. Her hands caressed the back of his neck and she smiled once they pulled away from one another.

"I love you," she said.

"I know," he replied. It was a response that she had become accustomed to. She had been with him for a long time and he never told her that he loved her. She didn't need him to say it, just to know how he felt. She was secure in their relationship and was confident that he had to love her. Why else would he spend cash on her or move into her apartment and pay all of her bills? Norelle didn't want for anything and as long as he kept her satisfied, she could live without hearing those three special words. She wasn't a child and her fairy-tale dreams of prince charming had been long gone. Kasheef was as good as it was going to get when it came to a thug and that was the only type of man that she wanted, so she accepted him as is.

"I'm tired, I think I'm going to take a shower and a nap before I get into this whole cruise thing," Norelle said. "Will you be too upset if I relax for a few hours?"

"Nah do you ma. I'll probably crash with you after awhile. I'm going to go find a bar and have a drink or two to get my mind right. I'll come and check on you in an hour or two," he responded.

Kasheef left the room and walked through the corridors of the ship toward the main deck. There were people everywhere and Kasheef had to admit that he could get used to a lifestyle like this. Kasheef had plenty of money, but never took the time to enjoy it. He wasn't in the streets or running the streets like most hustlers. He *was* the street. He controlled every corner, every dice spot, every ho stroll . . . everything belonged to him. He was like the landlord, leasing out his properties, making niggas pay rent. If you wanted to work his blocks, you paid rent. If a ho wanted to walk on his stroll, she paid rent. He even had local businesses giving him a percentage of their profits. Needless to say, he was a very rich man. His wealth went unnoticed though because of his low key demeanor and he had much love in the streets, but just like Biggie said, mo' money brought about mo' problems. He had to keep a handle on his hustling lifestyle which is why most of his time was spent in the streets. As the boat embarked on its three day journey, Kasheef finally located a bar.

"Can I get a Long Island Iced Tea?" he asked the bartender.

"Can you make that two?" a feminine voice beside him asked.

He focused his attention on the young woman standing next to him. Five foot five with an hourglass shape and caramel skin; she was easy on the eyes. Dressed professionally in a knee length skirt and a silk sleeveless top, she exemplified intelligence and sophistication.

The bartender brought back their drinks and Kasheef pulled out a wad of money to pay for both drinks. "Hey my man, here you go," he said as he placed a twenty dollar bill on the bar top. The woman looked at·him quizzically and smiled.

"You know that the drinks are included right?" she asked.

"Nah I didn't actually. I guess I just gave my man a nice tip," Kasheef replied.

The woman sipped her drink and said, "I guess so. Thank you for the gesture however . . . I mean if the drinks had not been on the house."

Kasheef felt like she was trying to clown him, but he had to admit that by trying to flash his cash in front of her he had made an ass of himself. "I'm Carmen, by the way," she introduced as she held out her hand.

"Kasheef," he replied smoothly and shook it gently.

"What brings you on this trip?" she asked nosily.

"I'm running from the New York winter," he stated, not wanting to give away the fact that he was actually on the boat with his girlfriend. He knew that he wouldn't be able to do anything with the girl next to him, but he was having a good time flirting with her.

"I'm from New York too!" she exclaimed. "What part?"

"Long Island, what about you?"

"Manhattan," she said.

"Manhattan? You look like a Manhattan woman," he stated with a casual smirk.

"Excuse me?" she asked with one hand on her hip.

"Nah ma, it's not a bad thing. You just look like you got your shit together nah mean? Like you one of them independent sisters . . . you know good job, more business suits than mini skirts in your closet, and no time for a man anywhere in that picture."

Her silence indicated that he was speaking the truth.

"Am I right?" he asked, already knowing the answer to the question.

"Shut up," she responded with a smile. She hated to admit to the handsome stranger that he had summed up her entire life perfectly. He had hit the nail on the head. Carmen had always been a woman who chose the career track over the social one, but because of it she was now without a man while most women her age had partners that they could settle down with. It was the one thing that was missing from her life. She had focused on being an independent woman for so long that now she yearned to know what it was like to be able to depend on a man. She wanted to go to sleep and wake up to the same face everyday. She wished for a significant other that could welcome her home from a hard day at work. She had not realized what a great sacrifice she was making until one day she looked up and all of her single friends were married with kids.

"Maybe we can change that one day," he said. Kasheef was charming and Carmen blushed slightly as a flattered smile took over her face.

She finished her drink and grabbed her purse. As she looked him up and down, definitely enjoying what she was seeing. "Maybe," she replied. "It was nice to meet you. Hopefully I'll see you around the ship." She walked away, being sure to put a little extra switch in her hips. She turned before she was out of eyesight and waved. She would've bet her life on it that he was watching her ass, but to her surprise he wasn't. "Maybe," she said to herself as she bit her bottom lip. She seriously entertained the thought of having a romantic rendezvous with Kasheef, but quickly talked herself out of it. *He is fine as hell though,* she thought silently as she shook her head and walked away in search of her cabin.

Kasheef retreated to his room where he found Norelle curled up on the bed. He sat down on the edge and stroked her hair. "Wake up," he whispered. "You gon' sleep the whole trip away."

"I know. I need to get up anyway." She sat up and stretched in bed. I have to get ready for the dinner."

After an hour of primping and switching outfits, Norelle stepped out of her suite looking flawless in white Ferragamo slacks with a visible crease, a white and gold Ferragamo halter, and gold Jimmy Choos. Her hair was pulled up off her face, showing off her exquisite features, the best one being her two carat diamond solitaires. Kasheef was clean in white linen slacks and shirt. His jewelry also accentuated his fresh look. She could tell that she looked good on Kasheef's arm because the envious looks of her sorority sisters said it all. There was nothing better than being the best dressed and best looking woman in a room full of other women. Her confidence was at an all time high as she glided through the room. It was important for her to make a good impression on her old friends. She knew that after the reunion was over that she would be the topic of many conversations and if they were going to talk anyway she was going to make sure that she gave them something to say. Her entire presence screamed new money, because the way that Norelle flaunted it was so blatant that you could not help but to see it.

Dozens of "hey girls" and "you look goods" floated through the room. Norelle had forgotten how fake a group of women could be. She was really only there for one person, but when she finally found her she thought she saw a hint of hater in her as well.

"Car—men!" she sang as she approached her from behind.

"Norelle!" she yelled out as she wrapped her arms around her long lost friend. Carmen's eyes diverted to Kasheef and a look of confusion crossed her face.

"Oh yeah! I'm sorry, I'm being rude. Carmen this is my boyfriend Kasheef," Norelle introduced. Kasheef and Carmen shook hands as if this was their first encounter.

"Nice to meet you," Carmen scoffed.

"Nice to meet you," he replied with a smile that just earlier she was hoping to see again. Carmen rolled her eyes, thinking that all men were exactly the same. Kasheef had flirted openly with her just a few hours ago despite the fact that he had a woman. She knew he was a player. His persona had been too good to be true. He was her friend's man and therefore off limits, but the restriction only made her envious of Norelle's relationship because Kasheef was most definitely easy on the eyes, and Carmen silently wondered what he may be like behind closed doors. Kasheef didn't even break a sweat and Carmen was amazed at how cool the man was under pressure.

"You look exactly the same! Oh my goodness it feels like it's been forever. How have you been girl?" Norelle asked.

Carmen shifted her gaze from Kasheef to Norelle. "I'm doing well. I'm just working—trying to make partner eventually at my law firm. What about you? Are the two of you serious? Any kids?"

Kasheef smirked, knowing that Carmen was trying to dig up dirt and find out just how serious his relationship with Norelle was. He licked his lips and played his role as loving boyfriend as Norelle answered, "No. No kids yet, but Sheef and I are very serious. Now you know I have never been a time clock punching type of girl. Kasheef is a good man and he takes really good care of me."

Carmen and Norelle fell right back into their rotation and caught up on each other's lives. It had been so long since they had the time to talk and that was a shame especially since they lived in the exact same city. Neither of them was surprised at how the other's life had turned out. Carmen had always been the level headed one, the responsible and dependable one. She had been driven in college and her pre-law major had become a reality quickly upon matriculation. Norelle was the party girl, the free spirit, the one who rode life's waves no matter how many times she wiped out. They were so different, which is why they were such good friends. Carmen discreetly questioned Norelle about her relationship with Kasheef, but once she heard how Norelle talked about him she knew he was off limits. They told Kasheef college stories and stayed up half the night with one another. Kasheef was glad that Norelle had found someone to occupy her time, because he had agreed to come on this trip for a reason. He had a goal to accomplish and he was going to need some privacy to do it. Norelle didn't know that his connect was located in Belize City, Belize; and that just so happened to be one of the stops on their trip. He was definitely not there for laughs and giggles. He was there for bricks and money.

Chapter Three

When the cruise ship finally arrived in Belize there was only thing on his mind—money. It was the first time he'd ever made the trip overseas to cop, so he was anxious to meet his connect face to face. The layover was only six hours so he had to travel into the ghettos and back by the time the boat took off. Kasheef's connect arranged for him to be picked up a couple miles from the highly publicized tourist area of the island. He caught a cab to the limo that was waiting on the side of the road for him.

"Welcome to Belize City, Mr. Solis is expecting you," the driver stated as he opened the door and Kasheef stepped inside. He saw the sandy white beaches turn into lush greenery. Paved roadways turned into undeveloped land as the driver made his way deeper and deeper into the island. Set back on top of a small mountain was a mansion unlike one he had ever seen. Its tall plantation-style pillars and beautiful marble fountain that sat in the center of the estate went beyond his hood rich statute. He was witnessing opulence and elegance. He wanted a piece of it. He stepped out of the vehicle and made his way up toward the entrance. The doors opened on cue and he was greeted by one of the sexiest women he'd ever seen. Her brown sugar colored skin looked good enough to taste and the warm smile that she greeted him with would have been enough to make him wife her. If there was ever such a thing as the perfect woman she would have surely been it, but his fantasy of whisking her away was cut short when she introduced herself as his connect's wife.

"Hello. You must be Kasheef. My husband is expecting you," she stated without giving her name. He followed her through the opulent house and into the back of the mansion where Osti Solis sat bird watching. His appearance was different than what Kasheef had expected. He was short and thin with olive skin and dark features.

"Kasheef, it's nice to finally meet you," Osti greeted with a handshake that was firmer than to be expected. His body seemed weak and scrawny, but the look in his eye was cold and calculating. "I'm not what you were expecting, eh'?"

"To be honest, you are not," Kasheef responded.

"The unexpected kingpin stays out of the radar. There are only two types of business men in this world: those who are in it for the money and those who are in it for the recognition. The ones who are in it for the money do not like to be flashy. The unseen can not be caught," Osti said, speaking words of wisdom that only came with years of success in the drug game.

"I agree," Kasheef conceded while nodding his head in understanding.

"How will you get the product back to the states?"

"Money talks," Kasheef responded.

"Indeed it does," Osti stated with a laugh. He turned his back to Kasheef and looked toward the sky to peer back at his birds. "Your shipment is already in the car. Leave the money with my wife. My driver will take you back."

"You don't want to count the dough? How do you know you can trust me?"

Osti turned back around with a smirk on his face and replied, "Fear creates boundaries for men. It controls what they will and will not do. The look in my eye stops you from crossing those boundaries. That is why I finally agreed to meet you in person. So I could look you in the eyes."

Kasheef nodded and retreated to the car, where twenty kilos of heroine sat wrapped in a duffle bag. Now all he had to do was figure out how he was going to get them back on the boat.

Kasheef exited the vehicle with the duffel bag in hand. He scanned the beach suspiciously to make sure no one was watching him. He found a beach shop that sold life vests and approached it where a young teenage kid was working behind it.

"Hey yo', my man, you trying to make some money?" Kasheef asked.

Kasheef purchased twenty life vests from the beach shop and then paid the young worker two thousand dollars to give them out for free to the passengers on his cruise ship. Kasheef boarded the ship and watched as the other passengers followed behind him with complimentary life jackets in hand, but as soon as they made it through customs Kasheef stopped all twenty passengers and collected the life vests from them. He told them that Belizean products were not tested as suitable floatation devices. After telling them how unsafe the vests were and compensating them with twenty dollars each for their troubles, he was able to get the vests off of their backs with ease. They had no idea that each vest's stuffing had been removed and replaced with a kilo of

Heroine. It was the only way that he could have gotten the drugs on board and although it was risky; it had worked like a charm. He quickly stuffed the life jackets back into his duffel bag and hurried to his room. He'd gotten dope past customs and was home free. He stuffed the entire bag underneath the bed and flopped down on top of it. A smile of satisfaction crossed his face. Norelle was exploring the ship with Carmen. He had gotten away with the impossible and the cruise ship was ready to make its return to the states. He couldn't have been happier.

"It was so good seeing you," Carmen said as she hugged Norelle affectionately. It was the final night of their cruise and they had just finished dinner as they prepared to settle in for the night. Both of them had tears in their eyes as if they'd never see one another again.

"What are we crying for?" Norelle said as she wiped her eyes and laughed. "We both live in NY. There is no excuse for us to go this long without talking again. I had fun. It's been a long time since I've had a close female friend."

"Well here," Carmen replied, pulling out one of her business cards. "It's my card. You can call me anytime. We'll do a weekly girls night out or something."

"Okay girl. Have a safe trip home tomorrow."

The two women embraced again.

"Yeah you be safe too. You better use that number," Carmen said as she opened the door to her cabin. "We'll get together sometime soon."

Norelle blew Carmen a quick kiss and retreated to her luxury suite where she found Kasheef passed out in the bed. She snuggled up underneath him and enjoyed the sway of the boat as it glided through the Atlantic Ocean. The setting was so romantic, the atmosphere perfect for a couple in love, but she hardly even saw her own man the entire time they were there. They were both preoccupied, her with old friends and he with his business. She admired him as he slept. He looked so peaceful, so content. She thought of the events that had occurred directly before the trip. She hoped and prayed that the drama was over because tomorrow it would be back to the real world.

Chapter Four

It had been four days and Alija still couldn't shake what had happened. She cradled her daughter against her chest as she rocked back and forth. She looked down at her baby and smiled when Nahla cooed back at her, the child's eyes sparkling like a pool of rejuvenating innocence. Baby Nahla was the most important thing in Alija's life. She was all that her mother had to hold onto. Nahla was the only consistent and unconditional love that Alija had ever had. Her entire world revolved around her child and her life was not her own, because she lived to make Nahla happy.

"I know baby girl. Mommy's not going anywhere, I promise. Nobody can take me away from you," Alija said lovingly as she thought of how badly the situation at the club could've ended. It made her look at her life in a new light. Alija loved her daughter more than anything in this world and they were all that each other had. She had never felt a love as significant as the one

she felt for Nahla. The emotional connection
between mother and child transcended all others and she felt guilty for jeopardizing her own
safety. Nahla needed a mother, a good mother,
and Alija planned on becoming just that. Her
club hopping days were a thing of the past. From
this day forward she would try to better herself
so that she could enjoy every moment in raising
her child. Alija placed a bottle of baby formula
in a pot of boiling water and placed the baby in
her swing as she sat down at her meager kitchen
table. Late notices and shut off warnings cluttered
the space in front of her. It didn't matter how
many times the companies sent her the letters;
they weren't getting their money because she
didn't have it. Alija was a product of the ghetto.
A welfare baby who grew up to become a welfare
mother, she had nothing. She banked on her
government checks that came on the first of each
month and gladly accepted them. They were the
reason she did not look for a job because she felt
as if she did find a job, her monthly checks would
stop coming and they would decrease her food
stamps so she was better off depending on the
state. A nine to five she had never had, but she
always had some type of hustle. Whether it was
doing hair, boosting clothes, or hustling men; it
didn't matter. Anything was game as long as it

helped her keep money in her pockets and food on her table. A tear escaped from her eye as she thought about what she had been through in the past couple of days. It had put a fear in her heart that she had never known and she knew that she had to do something. It was her responsibility to provide for her family and keep her daughter safe. She needed some money so that she could move her daughter out of the hood and start a new life for them both. Nahla's hungry cries erupted throughout the room, signaling Alija to check on the bottle. She removed it from the boiling water, tested the temperature on the back of her wrist, and then scooped up her daughter. "What am I going to do baby girl? We all we got, mama." Her daughter greedily sucked the bottle and Alija smiled as she carried her daughter in her arms as she went to check the mailbox. She was waiting on some paperwork from the state. She had a scheme brewing and she was anxious because it would put some extra money in her pockets. She had convinced her caseworker to give her a $1200 car voucher. The car that she currently owned wasn't registered in her name, so it wasn't hard for her to get the naive white woman to issue her a car credit. She already had one of her girls lined up ready to purchase the voucher for $800 cash. It was a quick way to make some easy money. She never even worried about the repercussions of her actions. It was her way of working the system, but she was tired of depending on the system altogether. She was looking for her way out she just hadn't found it yet. She carried the mail back into her apartment and frowned when she saw something addressed to Mickie from the US Department of Justice. "Oh shit," she mumbled as she lay Nahla down on the couch for a nap. She hoped that her sister hadn't gotten caught up trying to defraud the welfare offices. She knew that if Mickie got caught she wasn't going down alone. She'd be the first one coming to Alija talking about "Girl they got us." Alija quickly opened the letter and a sigh of relief escaped her once she saw what it was. It was only a request for Mickie to appear for jury duty selection at the end of the month. She put the letter in her sister's room and then went back to sorting through her bills trying to figure out which ones she could afford to pay this month.

"Ooh right there Sheef," Norelle moaned as her man's muscular body rested atop of her own, moving in a slow rhythm. His body was so toned and dark. The way that he was making love to her made her back arch and her toes curl. "I love you," she whispered as she rolled onto her stomach, changing positions so that he could enter her from behind, while she played with her feminine pearl. Kasheef admired Norelle's perfect body before filling the space between her legs. He rocked in and out of her, while kissing the nape of her neck all at the same time. He felt her body quiver as she reached bliss and with a few deep strokes he joined her in satisfaction. Norelle immediately turned on her side and fell asleep while Kasheef arose to take a shower. After washing his muscular body briefly, he went into the living room and turned on the TV. He couldn't believe what he saw.

"This is Sunshine Miller reporting live for NY1 News. This is the scene where a vicious murder was committed only a week ago. Ahmad Simmons' body was recovered yesterday by two fishermen who found the deceased floating face down in the Hudson River. After tracking his whereabouts with friends and family the police were lead to this night club. It is in fact the last place Ahmad was seen alive. The following tape that we are about to air has just been released by the New York City Police Department."

Kasheef's jaw hit the floor when he saw a videotape of the inside of his club. It showed himself and Ahmad inside of the office with Alija in the background peeking through the door. Kasheef's heart felt as if it would beat out of his chest as he watched himself shoot Ahmad on the local news station. It then showed him run out of the room after Alija and later showed three of Kasheef's goons come to clean up the murder scene. Luckily for Kasheef his face was not recognizable, but to his dismay Alija was easy to identify and he instantly regretted letting her walk out of the club alive. She was the only person who could identify him as the shooter and he was sure that the police would be looking for her. That only meant one thing—he had to get to her first.

Alija dropped the remote control as she listened to the news broadcast.

"The extent of this crime is so drastic that the police have released this private footage in order to find citizens who may have any information regarding this offense. The police are asking for help in solving this brutal murder. The NYPD have confirmed that the victim was a suspected drug dealer, so it is a very good possibility that this is a drug related murder. If you know anything that can help in their investigation or if you recognize anyone in this video, please contact the police at (212) 965-0800.

Funeral services will commence tomorrow night for Mr. Simmons. The public is welcomed to attend. Back to you Bob."

"Oh my God," she stated. The ringing of her phone caused her to jump.

"Hello?" she answered her voice barely audible.

"What in the fuck did you get yourself into? I just saw your face all on the news. Is that what happened the night you came in crying?" Mickie asked. She was talking a mile a minute.

"I don't know Mick . . ." Alija responded nervously. Tears swelled in her eyes and a huge lump formed in her throat. "I don't know. I was there and it all happened so fast. I just panicked. I saw him get killed."

"And now the whole world knows it," Mickie stated.

"What am I gon' do?" Alija asked.

"You gon' lay low that's what. Just chill out and don't say nothing to nobody. You've still got to live in the hood. You ain't got the money to get out so don't let them pigs talk you into snitching. You've got my little niece to think about. I'll be home in a couple hours. We'll talk more then," Mickie said.

"Okay," Alija answered before hanging up the phone. She went into her bedroom, grabbed her baby from her crib and lay in bed. Her skin crawled as she thought about how her life had just taken a turn for the worst, and for some reason she was afraid to turn out the lights. She stared at Nahla and knew that she was in danger. "I've got to get us out of here baby girl . . . soon."

"Yo', as soon as these lights go out we're in there. Hit everything moving. Sheef said he'd rather be safe than sorry so shorty got to go," Stick instructed as smoke from the blunt he was smoking escaped from his full lips. He sat outside of the apartment building with two goons behind him. They were there to do a job; to exterminate a problem. They were all working on behalf of Kasheef and knew the importance of what they were about to do because they were the same boys who had cleaned up the murder scene at the club. Their asses were on the line as well, so they had to do the job and do it right. Stick popped the magazine into his 9 mm pistol as he leaned his seat back and watched the building.

"Let's just do this. I ain't sitting here all night yo'," one of the dudes complained.

"Sit ya' ass down fam. When the lights go out, we go in . . . and not a minute before," Stick replied.

***

Alija couldn't keep her eyes open any longer. She slowly arose from her bed and flicked the lights as she prepared herself for a restless sleep. Nahla began to whimper beside her and she looked over and stroked her chubby cheeks. "What's wrong mama? Huh? You want your binky?" she asked lightly. Alija arose from her bed and tucked Nahla in snugly so that she couldn't roll off then went to retrieve her daughter's pacifier. She had to move quickly because she knew she would never get any sleep if Nahla got cranky. She made her way down the hallway where her daughter's diaper bag was sitting by the front door. "Shit!" she mumbled as she stubbed her toe on her coffee table while making her way through the dark. She bent down to grab the bag, but froze when she heard voices outside her front door.

"Kill everybody in this mu'fucka. We're not leaving any witnesses."

Alija's breath caught in her throat as she put the strap of the diaper bag across her body. She peeked out the door hole and saw three men standing outside with guns in hand. She sprinted back to her room, knocking into furniture on the way. She heard the lock to her front door click and the door open and close, but she didn't look back. She ran for her life until she reached her room. She knew her house better than her assailants and was able to make it to her daughter before they figured out which way she'd run. She closed and locked her bedroom door, then grabbed her daughter off the bed, trying her best not to make her cry.

Nahla began to whimper and Alija rocked her as she looked back and forth around the room trying to figure out where she could run.

"Shh! It's okay," she whispered as silent tears graced her face. *What the fuck am I gon' do?* She asked herself. All of her windows were barred so that wasn't an option. She remembered the crawl space above her bed. It was only a small attic like space and she wasn't even sure if she would fit inside, but she had to try. She jumped on top of her bed and reached up to remove the ceiling tile. She hurriedly placed Nahla inside first before she hopped up herself, the diaper bag still hanging from her body. Just as she slid the ceiling tile back in place, her bedroom door came crashing down.

"Bitch where are you?" one of the men yelled as he snatched open her closet door. He created so much noise that she felt Nahla stir.

God please don't let her wake up. Please, she prayed as she put her hand over her baby's ear and brought her closer to her chest.

"Kill all that noise," Stick instructed. He looked

toward the window. "The bitch got bars on her windows so she's in this mu'fucka somewhere. Find her."

Alija slowly rocked her body back and forth as she heard the men tear up her house, overturning furniture and all in their attempt to find her hiding place. Alija was terrified and she didn't know what was going to happen. She feared for the life of her daughter and she only hoped that the intruders would give up their pursuit. She heard their footsteps travel into the living room and her heart froze when she heard a knock at her front door—

Knock! Knock! Knock!

She heard her intruders panic.

"Oh shit! It's the police fam," one of them whispered.

Knock! Knock! Knock!

"Open up! NYPD!"

It was the first time in her entire life that she was happy to have the police at her house. She stayed in her position quietly contemplating her next move.

"Sit down and act normal . . . hurry up and turn this furniture back over and stash them pistols," she heard one of the intruders whisper harshly.

Stick opened up the door and greeted the police, "Hello officers. What can I do for you?"

"We had some complaints from some neighbors about a disturbance," one of the officers replied as he stood firmly in the doorway with his hand positioned on his gun holster.

"We probably did get a little loud officer. You know how it is when you get together with the fellas. I apologize," Stick answered, laying it on thick.

The police officer looked around the group of men suspiciously. "Is there anyone else in the house?"

Stick could've shit himself when he heard the female voice behind him say, "No sir, it's just me and my daughter's father and a couple of his friends." She walked out of the room with her daughter held snugly in her arms. Her eyes darted wildly around the room as she tried to remember the faces of the men who had come to do her harm.

Stick shifted uncomfortably in his stance as he stared a hole through Alija. The officer immediately recognized her face.

"Ma'am can you come with us please?" the officer asked. "You are wanted for questioning in relation to a murder that happened about a week ago."

"A murder? My girl don't know nothing bout' a murder, officer," Stick answered as his forehead began to sweat.

"I can come with you," Alija said eagerly, while silently thanking God for showing her a way out.

The officer nodded and responded, "You may want to leave the child with her father miss."

"My daughter goes where I go," she said harshly. "Now, I'm ready to make a statement."

She walked out of the apartment with Stick grilling her as she walked past. He was lucky she didn't turn him and his friends in. He smirked once he realized the game that the girl had just run on him and his crew. He respected her gangsta though, because she didn't snitch him out. He just hoped that she lived by the same code when it came to the murder.

"What was that?" one of the goons asked.

"I don't know fam, but let's get the fuck outta here before our luck runs out."

Chapter Five

That was so stupid. I should've turned them in. They are only going to come back for me, she thought regretfully to herself. *They're probably watching my crib right now . . . I have to warn Mick.*

She tapped her leg against the floor rapidly, while holding Nahla in her arms. The police had contained her in a questioning room for over an hour now and she just wanted to get this over with. She wasn't a snitch, but she planned on telling what she knew in order to protect her daughter. The door finally opened and a tall lean man stepped inside the room. He was dressed casually in slacks and a blazer, his badge hanging from his belt on display.

"Hello Alija, I'm Detective Nielson," he introduced. "Do you need anything? Are you hungry?" His voice was friendly but Alija was no dummy. She had been born and raised to hate the police so she knew he was playing the good cop role, she just wondered where the bad cop was hiding. "Can you tell me what you know about the night of March twenty-first? What happened at Club Blaze that night?"

Alija was quiet and her attention was on her child. She was hesitant to look at the detective and she sighed deeply.

"We know you were there Ms. Bell," he said, using her last name.

"His name is Kasheef, he owns the club," Alija said in a low tone.

"Is he my shooter?" the detective asked eagerly as he leaned into the steel table.

Alija nodded.

"And you will testify to that?"

"If that is what it takes to protect my daughter then yes. Now I need to call my sister."

Kasheef held Norelle in his arms as an uncanny feeling suddenly swept over him. He sat straight up in bed and looked around his room. It was too calm inside of his bedroom. It was as if the entire world had come to a standstill. He didn't hear the usual voices of the corner boys who were out trying to make a day's pay, or the sound of neighbors coming in from a late night out, even the hum of the refrigerator had ceased.

Everything was silent . . . too silent and the hair on the back of his neck stood straight up. He shook his head and told himself that it was just paranoia.

"What's wrong babe?" she asked as her brow furrowed with concern.

"Nothing, it's just too quiet in this mu'fucka," Kasheef replied, trying to shake the caution that his sympathetic nervous system was sending out. "Something just doesn't feel right."

Norelle pulled back the covers and revealed her naked, perfectly sculpted figure. "I know something that feels right. Come back to bed," she enticed as she opened and closed her legs seductively.

Kasheef crawled on top of her, their tongues intertwining in a passionate kiss, but they were interrupted by the hinges being knocked off of their front door.

Norelle and Kasheef jumped out of bed, but before they could do anything, their bedroom was swarmed with fully suited swat agents who held automatic weapons pointed their way.

"Get on the ground!"

"Get on the ground, now!"

"Kasheef?" Norelle screamed as she was hand-cuffed and put face down on the floor.

Detective Nielson approached Kasheef and slapped the silver bracelets around his wrists.

"Kasheef Williams you have the right to remain silent . . ."

"I want a lawyer," he said calmly and cockily as he cooperated fully with the police. He turned up his nose smugly and looked down at Norelle who was also being read her rights.

"Norelle!" Kasheef called out to her.

With her hair wild and her face stained with tears she looked at him. He shook his head from side to side and she already knew what the code meant. He was telling her to keep her mouth closed. Silence was the key when dealing with the police and it was something that the couple had discussed before, but talking about it and having it actually happen was two completely different things. Norelle could feel the panic setting in as she closed her eyes as the police slapped the cold, steel bracelets on her petite wrists.

Detective Nielson pushed him toward another officer and yelled, "Get him out of here!"

Before the officer could respond, another cop came into the room with a black duffel bag. "We've hit the jackpot," he announced as he unzipped the bag. The heroine that Kasheef had copped from Belize was packed neatly inside.

Kasheef instantly began smacking himself for keeping the product inside his crib, but he knew that it was a charge he could beat because the apartment was not in his name. The detective finished reading Kasheef his rights as he was escorted out of the building.

"I don't know anything!" Norelle screamed for the millionth time as Detective Nielson asked her the same questions over and over again. "Why are you doing this to me?" she asked. She was distraught. Her hair was a mess and the knot in her queasy feeling in her stomach made it feel as if her dinner would come up at any moment. The police detective was quickly backing her into a corner. She was trying to stay strong and not reveal what she knew, but with every threat Nielson threw her way, he chipped off a piece of her allegiance to Kasheef and she began to think of saving herself.

"You did this to yourself sweetheart. Dating a drug dealer must make you hot shit huh?" he grilled. He was leaned in so close to her that she could smell the scent of old tobacco on his breath and she had a front row seat to his crusty, crooked teeth.

Norelle was silent as she put her face in her hands and shook her head from side to side. She just wanted to get out of there. All she wanted to do was go home and forget that any of this had ever happened.

"Where were you the night of March 21, 2008?"

"I was at home," she answered.

"And where is home?" the Detective asked.

Norelle frowned and rolled her eyes, "Where did you arrest me at?" she shot back sarcastically. Her voice was full of irritation as she smacked her lips and sat back in her chair.

"So that is *your* apartment?" Nielson asked again, purposely repeating himself to make sure that he established her residency.

"Yes! How many times do I have to tell you? Yes, that is where I live," she replied. She had no idea that she had already said too much. The police were merely giving her enough rope to hang herself. With every word that she said she tied the noose tighter and tighter around her neck.

"Where was Kasheef on the same night?"

"I already told you he was home with me," she answered.

"All night?"

"Yes," she replied.

"What time did you go to sleep?" he asked.

Norelle didn't know how she was supposed to answer that question. She was growing frustrated and confused. "I don't know. I can't remember. Don't I get a phone call or something? I know my rights. You can not just hold me here like this. I want to make a call."

***

Carmen looked over at her night stand when she heard the irritating shrill from the ringing of her phone. "It's four o'clock in the morning. Who is this?" she said in exasperation. She picked up the phone. "Hello?" A sigh escaped her lips as she waited for a response.

"C . . . Carmen?"

Carmen sat straight up in her bed when she heard the distraught voice. "This is Carmen. Who is this?" she asked.

"It's me. I . . . it's Norelle."

"What's wrong? Are you okay?" Carmen asked.

"I'm in jail. I've been arrested and I need a lawyer. They're trying to get me to say things about Kasheef. I didn't know who else to call," she stammered.

Carmen threw the bed spread from her legs and hopped out of bed. She ran to her closet and pulled out a grey Donna Karan business skirt and silk blouse. "No, it's okay. I'm on my way. Don't say anything to anyone else until I get there okay?"

"Okay," Norelle said before the line went dead.

"What in the hell has this girl gotten herself into?" Carmen pondered aloud as she slipped into her clothes. She unwrapped her hair and combed it down around her face and slipped her feet into black three inch designer pumps. Grabbing her keys and her briefcase all in one swift movement—she ran out the door.

"You know you're going to go to prison right?" the detective taunted. "Twenty kilos of raw heroine inside your apartment. Whoo! That's a lot of time. You'll never get out and a pretty little piece like you will drive the butch broads crazy."

"Those drugs aren't mine!" she protested.

"So they belong to Kasheef?" Detective Nielson asked feeling like the girl across from him was getting ready to crack at any moment.

As soon as Norelle opened her mouth to speak, the door opened forcefully.

"This interview is over," Carmen stated. "Let's go Norelle." She helped her friend out of her chair and then nodded toward Nielson. "Detective."

"Counselor," he replied with a head nod. He could've protested and held Norelle longer, but she wasn't the type of fish he was looking to fry so he let her walk for the time being. He wished he had even a minute longer with her because he had a feeling that she was getting ready to talk. "I'll be in touch," he promised.

Carmen stopped dead in her tracks, turned on her expensive heel, and stared directly in the detective's eyes. "If you need to speak with my client about anything be sure you call me first," she said in a professional but threatening way. She wrapped an arm around Norelle and ushered her out of the precinct.

"Carmen I don't know what to say. Thank you," Norelle said once they were outside.

"Don't worry about it. Go home, get some sleep, and we'll meet for breakfast tomorrow morning to discuss everything. By then I'll have a lot more information about what they are charging Kasheef with and what they may be trying to charge you with."

"Can you get him out?" Norelle asked despondently.

"Not tonight, but that's what we'll work on tomorrow. Go get some rest girl. You're going to need it," Carmen suggested. The two women embraced and then went their separate ways. Norelle had the weight of the world on her shoulders and Carmen a huge smile on her face. She needed a major case like this. More importantly she needed to win a case like this. She was trying to make partner at her law firm and a case like this could make or break her career. She just hoped she was ready.

***

"What am I going to do?" Alija asked. "They could've killed me and Nahla."

"But they didn't sis; that's what's important. Thinking about what could've happened will drive you crazy," Mickie comforted as she held her baby niece and paced the floor of the motel room Alija had checked into. "You can't go back to the apartment especially now that you're snitching."

"Thanks Mick! That helps," Alija responded sarcastically. "What other choice did I have huh?"

"I'm just saying Alija. You don't even have any cash to relocate. You can't snitch on somebody like Kasheef and then go back to the hood thinking shit gon' be gulley. His people gon' be gunning for you just off of GP," Mickie said.

"Well either way I'm losing. He sent them dudes up in my crib before I said one word to anybody. I had no intentions of going to the police," Alija objected.

"It's done now. You've already started telling. Now you need to think about how you gon' live after all this is over. This ain't a game."

"No, it's definitely not that," she responded as she looked at her daughter. "This is my life Mick . . . it's her life."

Chapter Six

Carmen walked into her office to find her boss sitting in her chair. She was surprised and greeted him hesitantly as she sashayed toward her desk with a copy of the morning *New York Times* tucked beneath her arm.

"Good morning Richard," she said as she sat her Dooney & Bourke alligator skinned briefcase near her feet.

"Carmen . . . I hear you've taken on a major case," he stated.

"What case might that be?" she asked, unsure of what he was speaking of. Richard stood up from her desk and stepped out of her way as he motioned for her to take a seat. He reached for the remote control that controlled the small plasma television in her office. Flicking on the screen he turned to the local news station, catching the middle of the broadcast.

Kasheef Williams' arrest occurred early this morning. A police representative states that they are charging Mr. Williams with second degree murder. By obtaining a noted defense attorney by the name of Carmen Rose, it is definitely not an open and shut conviction for the prosecution. Ms. Rose is a junior associate at Barnes & Baker Legal Firm in Manhattan and has not lost a case in the five years she's been practicing law . . .

Her boss turned off the TV before the broadcast could finish playing and looked her in the eye. "Are you sure you want to take on a case of this magnitude?"

Carmen fidgeted in her seat. It was true, she had never lost a case but her record was jaded because she had never defended a crime more serious than aggravated assault. Murders, rapes, and drug related offenses were usually handled by the senior partners . . . more specifically the white male senior partners. She was up for evaluation in six months and she desperately hoped to be considered for the open position of senior partner. With her record she had a good chance, but her competition was sure to argue about the ease of the cases she'd previously tried. She needed to take a chance on a major case. Kasheef's case had just happened to fall into her lap. "Yes, Richard, I'm sure."

"Okay then . . . I can say this off the record. If you bring this win in for the firm, I can almost guarantee that the board of trustees will elect you as the new senior partner. You have full access to all resources and any paralegals or research teams you may need."

A huge smile crossed Carmen's face as her boss turned to leave. Before he exited fully he faced her once more. "But if you lose Carmen, it will set your career back five years. Everything you've accomplished will be overshadowed by this loss."

"I guess I have to win then," she stated confidently. Dawn walked into the office with an incredulous look plastered on her face.

"Is what they're saying on the news true? Are you really getting ready to defend Kasheef Williams?" Dawn asked.

"I guess so," Carmen replied with a slick smile. "If I can pull this off I'm taking you straight to the top floor with me Ms. Executive Assistant." She got up from her seat and glided past her secretary. "I'm going to meet with Kasheef's girlfriend to discuss her involvement in his activities. After that, I'm going downtown to let Kasheef know I'll be taking his case. I still haven't spoken to him yet."

Carmen made her way to Starbucks on Lexington Avenue and ordered two caramel macchiatos as she waited for Norelle to show up. Ten

minutes passed before Carmen saw her friend
come through the doors. She waved her over and
instantly felt bad when she saw Norelle's swollen
red eyes. She could tell that her girl hadn't gotten
much sleep.

"Thanks for coming," Norelle said while pulling out a chair and graciously accepting the
macchiato. She shifted in her seat nervously
and then looked up at Carmen. "I can't go to jail
Carm. I'll do whatever I have to do to get out of
this situation."

"What exactly is the situation?" Carmen asked.
"If I'm going to represent you, I'm going to need
to know everything. You can't keep anything
from me."

"Kasheef wasn't home that night Carmen. He
didn't come home until like four in the morning.
There was blood on his shirt," Norelle admitted.

"Do you think Kasheef committed this murder?" Carmen asked as she took notes on a legal
pad.

"Yeah, I do." Norelle was ashamed to say it. She
had bragged and flaunted Kasheef in front of Carmen, lying about what Kasheef did for a living to
make herself look better. Now the truth had come
out and she was forced to admit the truth. She did
not want to tell Carmen about what had happened
that night. Kasheef had given her specific instruc-

tions to be his alibi, but she was so afraid that she was just looking for a way out of her predicament. She didn't care who she had to throw under the bus in order to do it.

"And the drugs?" Carmen asked.

"I didn't even know they were in the house," Norelle replied incredulously.

Carmen reached over the table and grabbed her friend's hand. "I need to go speak with Kasheef. Try to get some rest okay?"

Norelle nodded.

"I'll call you later," Carmen said before walking away.

"Williams let's go!" an officer yelled as he came and removed Kasheef from the bull pen, placing him securely in cuffs.

Kasheef stood without protest and was taken to a small interview room. He stepped inside and noticed Carmen sitting in front of him.

"Norelle sent me," Carmen explained. She turned toward the officer. "Can you remove the cuffs?"

The officer unlocked the handcuffs and left the room. Kasheef massaged his wrists as he sat down in front of Carmen. "Thank you for coming," he stated. The crease in his forehead and the way that his brow dipped low revealed his stress. "What do they have on me?"

"Kasheef I'm not going to lie to you. I don't like to paint a fairytale portrayal of any case just to sugarcoat what is happening. I would rather be upfront and honest with you so that there will be no surprises. I want you to know what to expect of my services."

"I respect that," he replied. "Just keep it real with me. What am I facing here?"

"This does not look good," Carmen stated frankly.

"I know . . . I know. My back is in a corner right now. You've got to get me out," Kasheef said with pleading eyes.

"They have a witness. This entire case relies solely on her testimony. I've seen the tape from the club that night. Your face isn't recognizable which works in our favor. I will play on that fact as much as I possibly can. She's the only person that can place you at the crime scene," Carmen said. She hesitated before continuing. "I need to know everything Kasheef. Don't try to hide anything from me. I'm a lawyer. If you want me to do my job effectively I have to know what went on that night. I have to know the complete truth, not just what you interpret it to be. Did you do it?"

Kasheef leaned across the table until he was only inches away from Carmen's face. "I'll tell you what I'm not gon' do . . . this time they're trying to stick me with. Get me off." His voice was low as he spoke but it did not stop the authority from being present in his words. Carmen understood perfectly. She knew men like Kasheef. At one time in her life she had been attracted to men just like him. He was a boss and he was used to being in charge. He never asked for anything from anybody. He demanded respect and instilled fear in the hearts of many. He was not the type of man that you could tell no and she understood this. She nodded, knowing that he would never admit his guilt. He didn't trust her enough to incriminate himself and she could understand why. His life was on the line. Her gut told her that he was guilty, but her mind told her that it didn't matter. She was going to do her job to the best of her ability. Whether Kasheef committed the murder or not was irrelevant. She would do all that it took to sway a jury into finding him innocent.

"Okay," she said as she closed her briefcase and stood to leave. "You're being arraigned later on this afternoon and we'll enter a plea of not guilty. I'll try to get the judge to set bail. See you in court."

***

Alija watched from her car as Ahmad's friends and family slowly scattered from his grave site. She didn't know why she was there, but she felt compelled to go pay her respects to him. She had seen everything that had gone down the night he was murdered. She wanted to get out. She wanted to shed tears over his grave, but something kept her rooted in her car. She knew that she was not welcome. She knew the full story. She saw Ahmad try to rob Kasheef and then in the blink of an eye the situation turned in Kasheef's favor and Ahmad was the one who ended up dead. The tears that tainted her cheeks were those of sadness, regret, and fear. Kasheef knew that she had witnessed his actions, yet he let her go. Now she was scared, running for her life because she was getting ready to testify and turn state's evidence. She looked in the back at Nahla who was sound asleep in her car seat. She closed her eyes as she thought of all the things that her daughter would miss out on because of the tragedy that their lives had become. *You can fix this,* she told herself. *All you have to do is testify against Kasheef. After the trial all of this will be over. You can just pack up and leave.* She knew that she didn't have much, but she was willing to go as far as a full tank of gas would take her just to get out of New York. Just as she pulled away from the curb, her cell phone rang.

"Hello?" she answered.

"They really fucked our apartment up," Mickie said.

"I know, tell me about it. Do you think it's smart for you to be there? What if they come back?"

Mickie scoffed and replied, "They're not looking for me. They want you and after all the attention they drew the first time they won't be trying to come back here. I'll be fine . . ."

"Okay . . ." Alija replied skeptically. "Oh yeah I forgot to tell you that the state sent you some papers. I set em' on your bed. Something about jury duty."

"Yeah okay . . . good looking out. I'mma get myself thrown out of that selection so fucking quick. What I look like sitting on somebody's jury all damn day," Mickie replied.

"I know right?" Alija replied. "I'll call you later. I've got to go get my mind right."

"Say no more . . . I'll come through later on with the la, after I figure out what's up on this jury bullshit," Mickie said before hanging up the phone.

***

"On the state charge of 2nd degree murder how does the defendant plead?" the judge asked.

"Not guilty," Kasheef said.

The judge looked toward the prosecution's desk. "Is the state prepared to proceed to trial?"

"Yes we are, your Honor," District Attorney Nancy Schwartz, replied.

"Okay then, jury selection will begin immediately. If the both counselors agree there is a jury pool taking place today at 3:00 P.M. This jury pool was originally for another case, but this case takes precedence. Jury selection can begin today. Now let's proceed to the matter of bail," the judge stated.

The DA stood and said, "The state is asking for a remand."

Carmen immediately stood to her feet and interjected. "Your Honor, that is completely unreasonable. My client has no prior record and does not pose a flight risk. He insists of his innocence and on his behalf I must ask for a personal recognizance."

"On a murder trial!" the DA said with mocking laughter in her voice.

Carmen knew that she was grasping at straws by asking for Kasheef to be released on nothing but his word, but it was all a part of her plan. If she low balled then when the state countered her offer it would be around the right ball park. Otherwise the DA would try to stick her client with a high bail and she was going to fight tooth and nail to prevent that from happening. "Your honor the state has nothing but circumstantial evidence against Mr. Williams. Their entire case relies solely on one woman's testimony." Kasheef smirked to himself as he watched Carmen in action. She was passionate about what she did and he was glad that he had her on his team. He was confident in her skill.

"She's an eyewitness!" the District Attorney shouted.

The judge banged his gavel and sighed. "Ladies there has to be a medium that we can come to." He paused and thought for a moment. "Bail is set at $200,000 cash or bond."

Carmen smiled as Kasheef was handcuffed.

He nodded her way and said, "Send Norelle down with that bail money. I want to be out of here like yesterday."

"This is some bullshit. They got me up in here for some damn jury selection," Mickie complained.

"It's not that bad," the lady beside her commented. "They pay you ten dollars an hour just to be here."

Mickie rolled her eyes, but perked up a little bit as she thought about getting paid for nothing. A young black woman and an older white woman entered the room. They were assigned numbers and then pulled into a small room one by one where the defense and prosecuting attorneys asked a series of questions to determine the jury. When Mickie's turn rolled around she walked into the room and took a seat. She wore Seven jeans under an ivory NY & Company pea coat.

"Please have a seat. I'm District Attorney Nancy Schwartz," the white woman introduced.

"Mickie," she replied as she sat down.

"And I'm Defense Attorney Carmen Rose," Carmen introduced. "You are here to be considered as a juror on a very high profile case. A man by the name of Kasheef Williams has been accused of murder. Does this case sound familiar to you?"

Whaaat? She thought to herself. *Ain't this about a bitch? I'm sitting here getting considered for Kasheef's case.*

"No, that doesn't sound familiar," Mickie lied. She didn't know why but she felt compelled to get on this case now that she knew all that it entailed.

"Mickie have you ever been arrested or involved in any illegal activities?" The DA asked.

Mickie thought of all the times she'd defrauded the welfare offices. "No, I've never done anything illegal."

"How do you think drugs have affected your community?" Carmen asked, trying to gauge if the young woman had any personal vendettas against drug dealers.

"I guess I don't really think about it," Mickie said. She tried to sound neutral on the situations so that she could appease both the prosecution and the defense. She felt like she was at a job interview as her palms began to sweat.

"When choosing between two sides, what do you base your decisions on?" The DA inquired as she stared intensely at Mickie through wire framed glasses.

"On the facts that I've been given. I try to keep things as real as possible," Mickie said.

The DA looked at Carmen who then said, "I have no more questions. Thank you Mickie, we'll be in touch."

Mickie stood and shook both of their hands then stood up to leave. She smiled as she walked through the decadent halls of the historical courthouse. She couldn't wait to tell Alija what had just taken place. They were in a position to turn the tables.

***

Alija and Mickie sat outside of the motel room smoking la, as Mickie described what had happened earlier that day. Alija thought that it was ironic that Mickie had gotten requested to sit on the same jury to a case where she was the prosecution's star witness.

"So what, have they picked you yet? Are you on the jury?" Alija asked as she took the dutch from her sister's finger tips and brought it to her lips, inhaling deeply. She looked back at the open motel door to make sure her daughter was still asleep.

"Nah, not yet. I'm just a consideration, but I played both sides of the field when they were asking me all the questions. If things go like I think they're going to go, I'll be getting something in the mail requesting me to come back."

"This is some crazy shit Mick. How we both twisted up in this web?" Alija asked as she laughed out loud.

Mickie began to laugh too as she draped one arm around her sister. "What the fuck is so funny?"

Alija really started cracking up once she heard Mickie's question. "What you laughing for if you don't know why I'm laughing."

"Bitch, I don't know," Mickie replied as she wiped the tears of laughter from her eyes. "This some good shit."

Alija smiled and blew out more smoke. "Yeah it is . . . cuz I don't even know why I'm laughing. Ain't nothing funny about my life right now."

"I've been thinking," Mickie said. "What if I get elected to this jury? You're the only witness in Kasheef's case. If you really look at it, we're holding his freedom in our hands."

Alija passed the dutch back to Mickie and looked at her with hazy eyes. "What you trying to blackmail him?"

"Not blackmail, I'm talking extortion. If you're testifying you're gonna need some get away money," Mickie said.

"I'm willing to bet he'll pay anything to beat this charge," Alija commented.

Nahla began to cry and Alija stood to her feet, dusting off her clothes before she went inside. Mickie followed close behind as she watched her sister pick Nahla up.

"What do you think?" Mickie asked.

"I don't know Mick. We could be opening up a whole new can of worms—creating new bullshit, and stepping into more problems," Alija said.

"You forgetting about what you saw? What you've been through?" Mickie said. "You probably haven't even thought about how this murder has changed you and Nahla's life."

"That's all I've been thinking about Mick! That's why I have to be smart. Nahla needs me. I'm all she has," Alija protested.

"And you need some money to get out of here once this is all over," Mickie urged.

Alija nodded. "Just let me think about it."

Mickie hugged her sister and said, "I love you girl. Everything is going to be okay, but you seriously need to get with this and jump on this opportunity. It's the only way you're ever going to feel comfortable again without watching over your shoulders. Make shit happen sis—don't let it happen to you."

"Yeah a'ight . . . I told you I'll think about. Just give me a little bit of time."

Chapter Seven

The next morning, Norelle popped open Kasheef's safe. She knew that he had both Swiss and Cayman accounts, so the money inside the steel safe was just the tip of the iceberg. Since Kasheef's arrest she'd been conflicted in her loyalties. A part of her wanted to stand by Kasheef. He was her man and Norelle did care about him. In fact she loved him, but she was quickly discovering that her feelings were only worth the dollar amount he spent on her. Kasheef had bought her affection by showering her with lavish gifts. When he was on top Kasheef was the most handsome man in the world to her. He was her everything and she was willing to do anything to keep him happy so that she could keep her spot as his woman secure. She loved money and he had a lot of it that he was willing to share with her so in turn she loved him, but he was in jail now and her relationship was on rocky ground. Her fear of being dragged down with him caused her to consider her options. She looked at the neatly stack bundles of hundred dollar bills. The safe was filled from top to bottom and she estimated that there was at least three hundred grand in the safe alone. If Kasheef kept this much money in the house she could only imagine what he had in his accounts overseas. She pulled out $25,000 and put it in her Birkin bag before heading out to go meet with Carmen. She arrived at the Manhattan law firm thirty minutes later and was greeted warmly by Carmen as she took a seat in the plush leather chairs in her office. She had to admit. She was impressed. Her girl was doing well for herself. She pulled out the money and placed it on top of Carmen's desk.

"Here's the first payment for Kasheef's case. I know that's only a quarter of it, I can bring back more if you want," Norelle said as she sat back and folded her legs.

"No, this is fine for now. I'll be sure to keep my time on record so that we can settle the balance later," Carmen said. "I have good news for you."

"What's that?"

"Kasheef can come home," Carmen stated.

Norelle smiled, slightly unsure if she was really ready for him to get out of jail. With Kasheef locked up Norelle had full access to his funds. There was enough money in that safe for her to relocate and start over, without the drama of Kasheef. With that much money she didn't need to find a new man to take care of her. She would be able to provide for herself. "Oh, okay. Well . . . when will he be getting out?" she asked.

Carmen removed the money from her desk and put in a manila envelope. She then put the envelope in a small safe behind her desk. "As soon as you can get $200,000 to post his bond. He can be out as soon as today," Carmen said.

"I didn't think the state allowed you to come out on bail in a murder case," Norelle said with a frown on her face.

"They don't. I'm just that good," Carmen bragged as she winked her eye playfully at her girl. "As long as Kasheef stays out of trouble and keeps his court dates while we're going through the initial stages of the trial, he should be able to stay out of jail. The fact that the state's evidence is weak helped him out a lot."

"Oh," was all that Norelle could manage to say.

"I have a press conference scheduled today. I'll bring this case to the public from the defense's perspective and paint him to be wrongly accused. It's always good to have the community behind him," Carmen stated.

"What about the drugs?" Norelle asked.

"That's a completely different charge and will be prosecuted under federal jurisdiction. The federal courts haven't even brought an indictment against Kasheef for that yet, so we'll just focus on getting him off for the murder right now," Carmen said. She noticed Norelle's disposition and frowned. "Smile, your man's coming home. All you've got to do is go down there and get him." Carmen stood from her seat and looked at her lady Movado watch. "I don't mean to cut this meeting short, but I've got to get out of here. The press conference starts in twenty minutes. Call me if you need me."

Norelle got up and walked out of the office. Her head was all over the place. She thought about the money that was in Kasheef's safe. He had more than enough money to post bail, but she had no intention of getting him out. *If he goes to jail, that'll leave me with nothing but time and opportunity to spend his money.* Murder carried a twenty-five year to life sentence. She'd have nothing to worry about if he was convicted. Norelle thought back over the last two years in which they had been together. She tried to manufacture times that he'd done her wrong or cheated on her. She thumbed through her mental rolodex searching for just one memory that could justify her actions. A time he'd hit her or belittled her. All she needed was one instance to give her a reason to take his money and leave him rotting in jail, but she couldn't come up with anything. Kasheef had treated her well and upgraded her tremendously when they started dating. She had not a need or want in this world because of his generosity. A twinge of guilt swept over her as she thought about all the times he'd made her smile. She knew she was wrong, but she didn't care. Money made her world go round, and now that she had an opportunity to back stab Kasheef, she was going to take it. *It's all in the game,* she thought as she made her way home.

"My name is Carmen Rose and as you know I am representing Kasheef Williams. Mr. Williams is innocent and my team of legal consultants are doing all that we can to exonerate him of these false allegations. Keep in mind that Kasheef Williams is an upstanding figure within his community. He has donated countless hours to shelters in Long Island during the holiday seasons and even financed a youth basketball team in his neighborhood. If you listen to the rumors that are circulating regarding Mr. Williams' involvement in illegal activities you will only be contributing to the corruption of these charges. Now, I will take any questions that you may have." Carmen was in rare form as she stood on the courthouse steps and smiled for the cameras from all of the major news stations. She answered questions from the press professionally and handled herself like the star that she was. She was bringing major coverage to Kasheef's case and knew that it would help them in the courtroom. The jurors were sure to have seen the coverage and she hoped that it would help to paint a pleasurable picture of her client. As the press conference came to an end, she walked toward the black Lincoln Town Car that was waiting curbside for her. She turned toward the camera one last time and said, "I hope that all of you outstanding individuals will use the media as a way to spread a positive light on Mr. Williams' situation. We don't want the public to sensationalize the lies and ignore the truth. Justice is what we are seeking." She watched the media eat up her words like steak and potatoes and then disappeared into the car. One of her paralegals sat beside her and looked back at the mass crowd of reporters. "Wow, you definitely got their attention."

"That was the point," Carmen replied as she melted into the leather seats and closed her eyes. "The prosecution is sure to respond. It will be cat and mouse, tit for tat, until opening statements. Let the games begin."

The first thing Norelle did when she got home was open the safe. She needed to know exactly how much money she was working with. She pulled out each bundle and admired each stack that was perfectly wrapped in rubber bands. She laid all of the money out on her bed and began to count. The smell of the money was like a narcotic to her senses; her fingertips tingled at the touch of each hundred dollar bill. It was a diligent task, counting that much money but it was one in which she welcomed. There was so much money in front of her that she lost count several times, but she never complained. She eagerly started from the beginning, making sure not to miss one bill. It was what she called a good problem. It took her hours and when she was done the grand total was $325,000. She was ecstatic. She brought a handful of bills up to her nose and inhaled deeply, smelling her newfound riches. She threw the money into the air and fell back onto the bed in sheer glee. "Aghh!" she screamed at the top of her lungs to release some of her excitement. She lay down in the bed, a feeling of triumph rushing over her body. She knew what men meant now when they said money made their dicks hard. In between her legs was soaking wet as she slid her finger inside her panties. Her phone rang, interrupting her from pleasing herself.

"Hello!" she said once she'd snatched up the phone.

"I have a collect call from Rikers Island Correctional Facility for Norelle Gibson. Will you accept the call?"

"Yeah, I guess," she answered.

Kasheef's voice filled the receiver. "Yo', Norelle you talked to Carmen?"

"I left her office earlier today," she said in an innocent tone.

"Why you ain't post my bail this morning? These mu'fuckas done shipped me from city lock up to Rikers Island all because you didn't handle that," Kasheef said, obviously irritated.

"I'm sorry Sheef. Carmen said that there were some papers she still needed to file, but that I could come bail you out first thing in the morning," she said, convincingly. "You know I wouldn't do you like that babe. I'm over here sick without you. I'm playing with my pussy right now." Her voice purred and she massaged herself gently as she closed her eyes and pictured Kasheef in her bed. She had to admit that's one thing he was good for.

"Word?" he asked, on the verge of an erection. He could picture her spread eagle on their satin sheets and the image was tantalizing.

"Yeah baby. I can't wait for you to come home," she whined.

"Then come and get your man then," he said.

"Don't worry boo, you'll be home first thing tomorrow," she assured.

"Yeah a'ight," he replied. "Keep that hot for me. I got to get off of this phone, but I'll be waiting on you—tomorrow Norelle."

"I got you Sheef," she said and then hung up the phone. "Yeah right nigga!" she yelled to herself as she continued to please herself. Her body tensed as she brought herself to an orgasm. When she was done she rolled over on the bed full of money, pulled her covers around her body and fell into the most luxurious sleep she'd ever had.

Alija watched the woman on the television as she portrayed Kasheef as a model citizen. Alija was disgusted and frowned as she thought of how he had ordered his cronies to run in her apartment. She knew that the young boys were on a ghetto execution mission and she thanked God that the police had shown up when they

did. A knock at her motel door startled her and
she pulled back the curtains in the room to see
outside. Detective Nielson stood with his hands
in his pockets and she opened the door to greet
him.

"Hello Alija," he said as he glanced nosily inside the room.

"No one is here but me and my baby," she said
as she motioned for him to come in. "What can I
do for you detective?"

Detective Nielson looked around the down-
trodden room and asked, "When's the last time
you got some fresh air?" When she didn't respond he continued. "Why don't you let me take
you to grab a bite to eat? There are some things
that I want to go over with you regarding the
trial."

Alija nodded and replied, "Okay. Just give me
a minute or two to get Nahla ready."

"I'll be waiting in the car."

Alija slipped her daughter into a knit sweater,
tiny jeans, and winter booties. It was freezing
outside and she wanted to make sure that Nahla
was warmly dressed. She put her in the car seat,
threw a blanket over top of it, and headed out to
the detective's car. After securing Nahla in the
back she hopped up front.

Detective Nielson took her to a nice Italian
restaurant on the Lower East Side. Dinner was

awkward and silence filled the air as the two ate together.

"How do you feel about testifying?" he asked her.

"Like a snitch," she replied bluntly.

"You are not doing anything wrong," Nielson replied. "People like Kasheef Williams deserve to be locked up."

Alija shook her head. "You just don't get it. Where I come from you don't snitch. You learn that from the very beginning. When you're little, nobody likes a tattle tale; when you're older nobody tolerates a snitch. I'm putting everything on the line to testify in this case, but right now I feel like I'm damned if I do; damned if I don't."

"This no snitching rule is what is keeping the inner cities from prospering. It is something that has been drilled into your heads, but it is a bunch of bullshit. It stops the good guys from winning," Nielson stated angrily.

"I guess it's just a difference of opinion," Alija said stubbornly. She did not expect the detective to understand. She did not doubt that the hood had trained her and programmed her a certain way, but she was sure that the state had trained the detective as well. They were from two different worlds; like oil and water the two did not mix.

"The prosecution will want to work with you before the trial. The DA needs to prepare you for the defense's rebuttal," Nielson said.

"That's fine," she said in a low tone. She looked up at the television that hung in the corner of the restaurant. Ironically, the exact same case that she and the detective were discussing was being reported on the screen. Alija stared at a picture of Kasheef on the screen. She stared into the eyes of the man she was expected to help put away. She picked up her baby who had begun to cry and she looked at the detective.

"Damned if I do, damned if I don't."

Kasheef was growing tired of sitting in prison. Another day had passed with no word from Norelle. He knew that Carmen had handled everything on her end because he had called her to make sure. *I'm trying to give this bitch the benefit of the doubt,* he thought to himself as he looked around the empty cell. He recalled his last conversation with Norelle. She hadn't showed him any shade. The words that she had spoken to him had seemed sincere, but he couldn't get rid of the nagging feeling in his stomach that something was wrong. During the entire two years that he had been with Norelle he had trusted her wholeheartedly. She had never betrayed his trust. He even tested her on numerous occasions, by leaving money around, or by simply leaving his cell phone sitting out in plain view. Her honest heart never allowed her to lift a dime that didn't belong to her and her confidence always made her bypass his cell without checking it to see who was calling her man. Kasheef almost felt guilty for assuming the worst in his girl, but her actions were causing his guilt to fade and his suspicions to grow. What he didn't know was that Norelle was only with him because of what he did for her. Now that he was locked up he didn't serve his purpose. She was a money hungry bitch who had slipped through his gold-digger radar and now she had her claws in his back.

His thoughts were driving him to his breaking point; he couldn't contain himself any longer. He had to find out why he was still sitting behind the thick brick wall. He walked out of his cell and stood in line for the phone. His mind was playing games with him, causing him to become enraged. He tried to control his temper; he didn't want his rage to get him into any complications with the other prisoners. He was well aware of his own strength and ruthlessness, so if any of the inmates ever stepped to him he would surely gain another murder charge. He had to remain cool and distance himself until he got out. He desperately needed to get out. Twenty minutes later, the line to the phone finally decreased and he picked up the receiver and dialed the operator.

"You'd like to make a collect call?" the operator asked.

"Yes," he replied.

"To what telephone number and to whom?"

"516-845-9812 to Norelle Gibson," he said.

"Hold please."

The line went silent for thirty seconds. The operator came back on the line and said, "The collect call was not accepted."

"What?" he yelled into the phone. "Nah, that ain't right. Maybe you dialed the wrong numbers. I'd like to place the call again."

The operator repeated the same procedure, placing another collect call. Kasheef waited impatiently until the operator finally said, "I'm sorry sir, the collect call was not accepted."

Kasheef slammed down the phone. "I see how this bitch trying to play me," he said to himself as he returned to his cell. He was more than livid. He was ready to kill Norelle and it was then that he knew she was not to be trusted.

"I have a collect call from Rikers Island Correctional Facility for Norelle Gibson. Will you accept the call?"

"Hell no!" Norelle said as she hung up the phone for a second time. She grabbed three fat stacks of hundred dollar bills and put them into her purse as she headed out. "I think it's time I got myself a new whip," she said as she hopped into her '04 Cadillac Escalade truck and drove to the dealership. By the end of the day she copped an '08 Lexus convertible coupe. She had also linked up with a realtor who was helping her shop for a brand new condominium. She already had the home furnished in her head. She had put deposits down on furniture all over the city, so that once she found a place all she had to do was have her furniture delivered. Norelle had her eyes on a specific place. It was taking her no time to blow through Kasheef's money. By the end of the day she had spent an easy seventy grand. She had never had that type of money in her possession in her life and now that she did, she didn't know what to do with it. She was on a shopping spree and for a woman as materialistic as Norelle, having that much paper to burn was like heaven. She couldn't remember a time when she'd been happier. Clothes, shoes, and cosmetics gave her confidence. Cars and jewelry made her feel important. There was nothing better to her than rolling through the streets having everyone notice her. Money distinguished her. It put her on an entirely different level than other women. *It's bum bitches at the bottom and Norelle at the top,* she thought arrogantly to herself as she made her way back to her apartment. She was enjoying her newfound wealth and once she spent the first dollar, all thoughts of it ever belonging to Kasheef were erased from her mind.

Norelle struggled with the many bags that she carried as she tried to find her keys to unlock her apartment door. Her phone began to ring on the inside and her frustration caused her to drop her bags. "Damn it!" she screamed. She decided to leave the bags where they were for the time being and sprinted to the cordless telephone.

"Hello?" she answered as she looked back at her front door to make sure her bags were still in the hallway. An old woman passing by stopped and eyed the bags curiously.

"I have a collect call from . . ."

Norelle stopped listening when the old woman reached into one of the bags. "Are these bags yours?" the elderly woman asked.

"Yes!" Norelle yelled as she shooed the woman away.

"Okay, I'll connect your call," she heard the operator say once she'd refocused on the telephone.

"Wait no! I didn't accept—" she tried to detest the call, but was interrupted by Kasheef's voice.

"Why you ain't taking my calls Norelle?"

"Baby I am. What are you talking about? You haven't called me since the other day," she said, trying to play off her deception.

"I called your ass two times earlier and both times you didn't take the calls," he said. "Bitch you trying to leave me in here on stuck? Where's my fucking bail money Norelle?"

"Kasheef, what are you talking about?" she asked as she tried her hardest to muster fake tears. "Nobody called me earlier! I would've accepted the charges, you know that. The operator must have dialed the wrong number. And I don't have the money to bail you out. The police came in here with a warrant and they took all of the money out of the safe!" She sobbed uncontrollably and put on a genius performance, one that might've gotten her an Academy Award if she had chosen to be an actress instead of a gold digger. "I'm out here trying to hustle up bail money for you and you're calling me on this bullshit."

"When did they run in the house Norelle?" Kasheef asked.

"Yesterday. I've been waiting on you to call so I could tell you. That's how I know the operator got the number wrong earlier because I would have accepted the call. I'm out here all by myself scared and worried everyday about you," she cried, adding a loud sniffle for dramatic effect while rolling her eyes in the mirror.

"A'ight ma," he said with a sigh. "Stop crying."

"I can't believe you would think I'd turn my back on you," she whispered.

"I don't think that Norelle. These walls are just fucking with my head. Look yo' I've got to get off this phone. I'll call you tomorrow, a'ight?" he asked.

"Okay," she responded and quickly hung up. She looked in her vanity mirror and quickly wiped away the fake tears. "Sucker ass nigga."

Mickie tore open the letter from the Department of Justice and jumped up and down when she saw the words 'YOU HAVE BEEN SUMMONED TO JURY DUTY,' printed in big bold letters. She knew that this could work to her advantage if she wanted it to. She picked up the phone and called Alija.

"Hello?" Alija answered.

"You'll never guess what I'm holding in my hands right now," Mickie said without even saying hello or stating her name.

"What Mick?" Alija asked, automatically recognizing her voice.

"The key to your future, baby sis," Mickie said matter of factly.

"If it ain't a million dollars then it can't open any doors for me," Alija joked.

"I don't know if it's worth a million, but it can damn sure get us some money!" Mickie replied. She couldn't contain the excitement in her voice.

"Girl what are you talking about?"Alija finally asked.

"I've been summoned," Mickie said.

Alija got quiet as she weighed her options. She really didn't have anything to lose. She was in a lose-lose situation so she figured that she may as well try and get some money to take care of Nahla. She didn't want to pull Mickie into it however.

"I'll do it. I'll blackmail him under one condition," Alija said.

"What is it? Anything," Mickie replied.

"You have to let me handle it. I don't want you involved Mick. If something does happen to me, I need to know that Nahla has someone in this world that will look after her. All I need you to do is sit on that jury and have my back when I need it, okay?"

"Okay Alija."

"And we probably need to distance ourselves for awhile. We can't be seen together at all. No talking to each other. We have to act like we don't even know one another until after this trial is over. I need you to be on that jury Mick. You are my ace in the hole in case something goes bad. If the jury is going to come back with a verdict that I don't like, I'm gonna need you on there to sway their asses in my direction," Alija explained. "When I get the money from Kasheef, you know I'm going to look out for you."

"I already know sis. I just wish that there was more that I could do," Mickie complained.

"You're doing enough already Mick. Just trust me. Don't contact me. We have different last names so no one will ever figure out that we are related as long as we are careful. My name isn't on your lease at the apartment so we should be good. Just keep everything quiet. I'll be in touch with you, okay?"

"Okay. I love you girl and be careful."

"I will," Alija answered then hung up the phone. Alija was scared because she knew that she was playing with fire. She kept telling herself that she had nothing to lose and everything to gain, but she knew that was untrue. She had her daughter to lose and the one thing that she didn't want to leave behind in this world was a motherless child. She hoped that God would see her through this. She had never been the religious type, but she knew that she could not do this alone and He was the only one that she could think of to call on. She grabbed her daughter in her arms, humbly got down on her knees and prayed.

Dear God,

I know you don't hear from me often, but I'm coming to you today. I'm burdened. My heart aches in a way that I have never felt before. My life is out of my hands. I feel like I'm losing everything and I need your help. For me to even be on my knees right now means that I need you. Nahla needs you. Please give me the strength to make it through this trial. I'm just trying to provide a better life for my daughter, the best way that I know how. Give me the courage to go through with this. Please.

Amen.

Chapter Eight

Beep! Beep! Beep!

Carmen sighed as she removed her sleek Fendi reading glasses and threw them onto her desk in frustration. She was trying to find a loop hole in Kasheef's case, but she was having a hard time concentrating. Every time she got focused another distraction caused her to slip up. If it wasn't the ringing of her telephone, then it was a knock at her door. This time it was the beeping of her intercom system.

"Yes, Dawn?" she asked dryly as she held the intercom button down.

"I have an Alija Bell here to see you," Dawn announced.

"Alija Bell?" Carmen asked as she tried to recall the name. Her eyes widened in surprise as she finally remembered where she had heard it before. "Alija Bell, as in the star witness to the Williams' case?"

"I believe so. She says she has some information that you may be interested in hearing," Dawn stated.

"Okay send her in," Carmen said as she closed Kasheef's case file and stood up to greet her guest. Curiosity was killing her. She could not imagine what the star witness in the biggest case of her life could possibly want, but she could not wait to find out. She walked from around the desk when the girl walked in and she immediately recognized her from the tape that she'd watched of Kasheef's crime. "I take it you are the woman that the prosecution has found to solidify their case?"

"That would be me," Alija responded as she extended her hand toward Carmen. Carmen looked skeptically at her hand and then shook it firmly.

"I'm not sure what it is I can do for you," Carmen admitted. "Technically you're not supposed to be here."

"It's not about what you can do for me, but what I can do for you . . . or more like Kasheef."

Carmen folded her arms and leaned against the front of her desk. "What could you possibly do for my client, Ms. Bell?"

"I could change my testimony," Alija responded frankly. Carmen tried to hide her shock behind her sophisticated demeanor, but Alija had just thrown her a curveball. Alija was the only person who was standing in her way of a victory and now here she was in the flesh, offering to switch sides. "We both know that I can identify Kasheef. He was there and he killed Ahmad, and unfortunately I'm the only one who saw it. I didn't ask to be put in this situation. I'm not in the business of ruining lives; I'm just trying to live mine."

"Why are you offering to do this now? What changed your mind?" Carmen asked, suspiciously.

"I was never going to snitch from the beginning. Kasheef started this when he sent his little workers to my house and make sure you tell him that. I'm just trying to come up with the best solution for both of us," Alija stated.

"I don't know anything about Kasheef sending anyone to your home Ms. Bell, but I'll deliver the message. What if I told you I didn't need you to change your testimony in order to get Kasheef off?" Carmen stated confidently.

Alija laughed before replying, "You're not that good. Let's be real. We both know that if I testify against Kasheef there is no way he will walk."

Carmen hated to admit it, but no matter how well she performed her job she felt like there was a great possibility that she would blow this case.

The defense was at a disadvantage and an offer like the one she was being given didn't come everyday. She needed this win. Her career depended on it. "How much is it going to cost him for your cooperation?"

"$200,000," Alija said.

"As you know, a matter like this is a sticky situation. I'm putting a lot on the line by even considering this. Just this conversation is putting my job in jeopardy. Don't misunderstand that what you are doing is illegal and if you are caught I will deny any participation in this arrangement," Carmen stated seriously in a low tone so that no one outside of her office door could pick up on the conversation.

"I understand," Alija said.

Carmen sighed deeply. "Let me discuss some things with my client and I'll get back with you. Is there a number where I can reach you?"

Alija shook her head. "No. Like you said this is serious business so let's not leave a paper trail. I'm staying at Motel 6 out in Long Island, room nine. If you need to speak with me come there and come alone. My offer is only good for forty-eight hours."

"I'll be in touch," Carmen stated as she finished writing down the information that she was just given. She put the pen down and opened her office door. Alija began to walk out. "Oh yeah . . . and Ms. Bell?"

Alija stopped dead in her tracks and turned around.

"Don't come to my office again. If you need to talk call me; I'll come to you." With that Carmen closed her office door. She couldn't believe the turn of events that had just taken placed. A sly smirk crossed her face as she thought of how her new office on the top floor was going to look.

Carmen walked out of her office and stopped at Dawn's desk. "Can you forward all calls to my voicemail? I need to make the trip to Rikers today and it'll probably be an all day trip."

"Sure, is there anything you need for me to do?" Dawn asked.

"Yes, actually there is, but I need you to be discreet. Find out as much information as you can on Ms. Alija Bell," Carmen said curiously.

"Sure, what case file would you like for me to put the information into?" Dawn asked.

"Just put the information in my right desk drawer. It's not for a case. I just need to know more," Carmen replied before walking out of the door.

***

Kasheef was relieved when his name was called. He knew that it had to be a visit from Carmen. It was the only time that the COs pulled inmates out of their cells without questions. He had been driving himself mad thinking about Norelle. He knew in his heart that the excuses she had given him were lies, but his pride hoped that he was wrong about her. He would be humiliated if his suspicions were confirmed and if she turned out to be a snake. He got up and walked slowly through the tier toward the front of the prison, until he came to a crossroad. To his left was the exit from the facility, to his right was the interview room where Carmen awaited him. He looked left for a second and hoped that he would one day be able to take that route. He walked in and as usual Carmen was stunning in her designer suit. Today she wore glasses which left an image in his head of a sexual fantasy he'd once had of a school teacher. He chuckled to himself and shook the image from his mind. He'd definitely been in jail for too long.

"Why are you still here Kasheef? Why haven't you posted bail?" Carmen asked in confusion as worry lines creased her forehead.

"That's what I'm trying to figure out," he replied. "Let me ask you something; Carmen and I need you to be honest with me."

"Go ahead."

"Have the police gotten any new warrants to re-search my home?" he asked. He stared her directly in her pupils so that he could try and detect a lie if one slipped from her pretty lips.

"No, why would you ask that?" she inquired.

"So the police haven't confiscated any new evidence?" he asked.

"No, they haven't. Honestly Kasheef, the police have more than enough evidence to make their case," Carmen said.

That lying ass bitch. I would have given her anything but she had to be greedy. She's trying to go against the grain and play me like I'm stupid . . . grimey ass bitch, he thought.

"Kasheef I have to talk to you about something. Something private that can't leave this room you understand?"

"Yeah, speak your mind Carmen," he said.

"Alija Bell stopped into my office today . . ."

"What?" he asked in exasperation.

Carmen looked around and leaned into the table inconspicuously. She lowered her voice then continued. "She told me to tell you that she would've never come forward if you hadn't sent your hit squad to her house."

Kasheef gritted his teeth as he listened to his lawyer speak.

"She says that she's willing to change her testimony on the witness stand and say that you are not the man that she saw shoot Ahmad Simmons," Carmen said.

"Does that mean I'll walk?" he asked.

"She is the key to the prosecution's case. Without her the murder charge won't have much to stand on. If she keeps up her end of the bargain, I believe we'll win. The judge may even throw out the case against you."

"What is our end of the bargain?" he asked.

"She wants $200,000 and we only have forty-eight hours to respond," Carmen said.

"Make it happen," Kasheef said. He stood from the table. "Thanks for everything Carmen."

"Don't thank me yet. This is far from over, but things are looking better for us," she said with a smile.

Kasheef returned her smile and then walked out of the room. By the time he got back to his cell it was recreation time. He immediately got in line for the phone. After a short wait he placed a call to his man.

"Yo', Stick!" he said once he was connected.

"Oh shit, I know this ain't who I think it is. What's good fam? How you holding up in there?" Stick asked.

"I'm good baby. Listen, I need you to come through with that bail money for ya' boy. It's twenty stacks, but you know I'm good for it. I'm just having a little trouble catching up with my chick, nah mean?' Kasheef stated.

"No doubt fam, I'll be there first thing tomorrow. I saw your girl pushing a new whip the other day. She showing shade now that you caught the case?" Stick asked, already knowing the answer to his question. He wasn't one to categorize all females into the same category, but bitches like Norelle never stuck around when the heat blazed. When things are good, champagne is flowing and money is long; they were happy, but as soon as it was time for their loyalty to be tested they ran dry. He had never cared for Norelle and could see through her gold-digging tactics, but out of respect for Kasheef he kept his mouth closed and showed her love. Now her true colors were bleeding through her cheap visage and Stick felt bad for his mans for falling into her trap. Many a nigga had been left broke behind some woman who had stuck them for their paper and gotten ghost when they were supposedly doing a bid with their man.

"Yeah, the shady bitch thinks she slick, but I got it under control," Kasheef said calmly. "Just make sure you come through a'ight?"

"Yeah I got you."

"One." Kasheef said and then ended the phone call.

Kasheef grinned to himself. He couldn't wait to hit the streets. He knew that he would have to lay low so he wouldn't be able to get at Norelle the way that he wanted to, but he was definitely going to see her. He had something else in mind for her however, something that she would never see coming. He also needed to settle a score with Alija Bell. He would pay her a visit too just to be sure about what the terms of their agreement really were.

Carmen placed a call to Norelle to inform her on the latest developments of the case.

"Norelle, I have some good news for you," Carmen stated as soon as her friend picked up her cell.

"What? You sound excited. What is it?" Norelle asked eagerly.

"I think your man is going to win his case. At first I was worried because the evidence against him was so concrete," Carmen stated.

"Well what the hell changed?" Norelle asked, coming off more harshly then she intended to. She needed Kasheef to be found guilty. She had already fucked him over. It was too late for her to turn back. She had lied to him and had already begun spending his money. She knew that her disloyalty was not something that Kasheef would be willing to forgive and although she had never seen his violent side, she did not doubt his gangster. She knew exactly what he was capable of and did not underestimate his ruthlessness. His hood status in New Yitty had been what had attracted her to him, besides the money, in the first place. Money. Power. Respect. To Lil' Kim it's the key to life . . . To Norelle it was the key to her heart and the treasure between her thighs, but those were qualities that Kasheef could not hold onto behind bars and because of his downfall Norelle had changed her locks. At one point Kasheef had it all and she had wanted a piece of the pie, but she knew that she had bitten the hand that fed her. Now she had to find a way to keep his ass locked up. *Why this bitch got to be so damn good at her job?* Norelle asked herself.

"The only witness in the case offered to recant her testimony," Carmen stated.

"She did what?" Norelle asked. "How did this come about?"

"The girl wants money, what else?" Carmen scoffed. "I talked it over with Kasheef and he thinks it's a good idea so we are going to go for it."

"Are you sure this is a good idea Carm," Norelle said trying to plant seeds of doubt and uncertainty in her girl's mind. "I mean I love Kasheef and I want him out of jail more than anyone, but isn't this illegal. Couldn't he get in more trouble for this? Better yet what about your law career. You could be disbarred!"

Carmen had already weighed all of her options. She knew exactly what was at stake, yet she was willing to take the risk. A career without advancement was equivalent to having no career at all so she was about to take her chances. With a victory from this case she would skyrocket to the top. Everything was about to blow up for her. Her career would be at an all time high. Salary. Ego. Benefits. The sky would be the limit. She would be her own boss.

"I've thought about all of that already Norelle," Carmen said. "Honestly, this is Kasheef's only shot at freedom. I know what I'm doing. You leave the law up to me and I'll make sure that your man comes home for good."

That's what I'm afraid of, Norelle cursed silently. "Well where is Sheef now?" she asked with a sigh.

"He's still locked up in Rikers," Carmen responded. She frowned and continued. "Why haven't you bonded him out yet Norelle? He doesn't look good. I mean he's not physically ill or hurt, but when I look at him I can see the burden on his face. It seems like he is carrying the world on his shoulders. He really needs to be home, you know?"

"Yeah I know Carm. I'm trying my best to come up with the money. Twenty stacks does not come easy these days. I should have the rest of the money by the end of the week. I planned on getting him out then," she lied as she rolled her eyes. "But listen how far away are you from the city? We can do lunch or something."

"I'm not close at all. I just left Rikers and I have some things I need to look into when I get back. I'm going to have to take a rain check."

Norelle bust a U-turn and headed toward Carmen's office. "Okay, well I'll call you later." She disconnected the call and threw her cell phone in her lap out of frustration. "Ughh!" she yelled as she hit the steering wheel repeatedly.

Fifteen minutes later, Norelle found herself pulling up in front of Carmen's workplace. She walked into her office as if she belonged and found that no one was sitting at the secretary's desk in front of Carmen's office. She let herself in and walked over to Carmen's desk. Her hands shook as she ruffled through the many papers and manila file folders that were scattered on top of the desk. She tried to hurry so that she could get in and out undetected.

"Where is it? Where is it?" she mumbled impatiently. She finally located Kasheef's case folder. She thumbed through it, quickly reading some of the details of the case. She located the name of the witness in the case. *Alija Bell,* she read as she went over a brief bio on the girl. *Now all I have to do is find you.* She continued to rummage through the papers until she found a piece of paper with Alija's address on it. It was for a motel and she figured it had to be what she was looking for. *I think I might pay this bitch Alija a visit myself,* she thought as she recopied the address on a piece of paper. She was just about to leave the office when she heard voices outside of the door. She saw the doorknob turn. *Oh shit,* she thought as she ducked underneath the desk and pulled her knees close to her body so that she would fit. Her heartbeat was erratic and her nerves shot as she tried not to breathe too loudly.

"I'd like to view the case file on Mr. Williams' case," she heard a male voice say.

"Sure, no problem. I'm sure Ms. Rose left it somewhere on her desk," a feminine voice replied and sat down in the chair. Norelle flinched as she tried to avoid contact with the woman's legs which were inches from touching her. She scooted as far into the small space as she could and closed her eyes, praying that they wouldn't find her. Norelle's eyes shot open in dismay when a pungent smell wafted up her nostrils. She almost threw up in her mouth when she noticed that the smell was coming from in between the legs of the seated woman. *This is what I get for trying to snoop,* she thought disgustedly as she took in as little air as possible. She felt like she was choking on rotten fish. *God please let her find this damn file before I die underneath this mu'fucka.* "Oh, here it is!" the woman announced and then the legs and deathly smell disappeared. Norelle waited until she heard the door open and close before she burst from underneath the desk, gasping for air. She was sure to return everything to its original condition then she snuck out of the office undetected, with a frown on her face.

"Mommy is gonna get us out of here baby girl," Alija said as she fed Nahla the bottle and watched TV. She was watching the local news to make sure that she was on point with what was going on in Kasheef's case. There had been coverage on it at least twice a day and she felt like she needed to

be involved of every aspect. She was attempting
to swindle a very dangerous man and she wanted
to make sure she was aware of the circumstances
surrounding the situation. She was nervous and
had been waiting on a visit from Kasheef's legal
defense. When day turned to night she feared
that maybe she had asked for too much money.
What if they don't pay up, she thought anxiously.
There was no guarantee that Kasheef would even
be interested in taking her up on her offer. *Maybe
I shouldn't have given his lawyer my address.
What if she gives my info to him? He can just send
some of his goons here again to finish me off,* she
thought. She noticed that her daughter's bottle
was empty. She put the baby over her shoulder
and gently patted her back while walking around
the room nervously. A car door slammed and she
walked to the window to see who was outside. She
didn't recognize the woman so she walked away
while still attempting to burp her child.

Knock! Knock!

Alija frowned. She answered the door and
stared into the eyes of a woman she didn't recognize.

"Can I help you?" she asked.

"Are you Alija Bell?" the woman asked.

"Who are you?" Alija replied as she looked the woman up and down, her arched eyebrows raised in defense.

"My name is Norelle. I'm Kasheef's girlfriend. Can I come in?" she asked as she shivered from the winter cold.

"No," Alija replied bluntly and began to close the door.

Norelle stopped the door from closing with her hand and shouted, "I want to pay you to testify against Kasheef!"

Alija's chin dropped to her chest and her eyes grew wide in surprise. "What?" she asked incredulously. "Did you say against him?"

"Can I come in? Please," Norelle asked again, this time almost pleading to gain entrance. She needed Alija to send Kasheef away to prison.

Alija moved to the side and allowed Norelle to step into the room. Norelle tried not to turn her nose up at the horrible accommodations.

"You can have a seat," Alija offered.

I'm not sitting my ass on that filthy chair. As a matter of fact, let me hurry up and get out of here. "No, I won't be long. I heard about the offer that you made to Kasheef's lawyer this morning. You see Carmen Rose is my best friend from college, which is why she chose to defend him. The reason why I'm here is because I need for you to testify."

Alija put her hands on her hips and interjected. "Look, I've already told your man's lawyer what I'm willing to do . . ."

"I want you to testify *against* Kasheef!" Norelle blurted out, interrupting Alija.

"What?" Alija asked in confusion. She had thought she had heard the girl wrong the first time, but she wasn't deaf or dumb.

"Yeah you heard me right. I would like to pay you to tell the jury what you saw that night," Norelle said.

Alija peered at Norelle. She didn't know if she could trust her. It was obvious that she had no type of loyalty toward Kasheef. *Her ass was probably living nice while he was out and doing good. Now he's locked up and she's trying to keep him in,* Alija thought in disbelief.

"Why would you want me to send Kasheef to prison?" Alija asked suspiciously. Growing up in the hood she could peep a fake bitch when she saw one and the girl in front of her was as phony as a Chinatown Coach bag. She did not have room to make any mistakes and she had to be extremely careful in the game she was trying to play.

"Look, it's not in my best interest for Kasheef to beat this case. I never expected him to come home. After he was arrested I ran off with some of his money and stopped accepting his calls from prison. He's sitting in there waiting on me to bail him out, but he'll be waiting for awhile if you know what I mean," Norelle replied frankly.

Alija turned up her face as if Norelle stunk. *This bitch is dirty*, she thought. *It's fucked up how she's trying to play him*. Alija was reluctant to deal with Norelle. She figured if she had turned on her own man then she definitely couldn't be trusted.

"I know what you're thinking," Norelle stated. "But I feel like no one can judge me but God. I know it seems bad, but I'm just trying to look out for myself. I can't think about Kasheef. Shit, he did not think about me! He chose to be in the streets and I know just as well as you that he killed that man. That's on him. I refuse to suffer behind his bullshit. I can't do that time with him. I'm not the one to be stressed and making monthly trips to Rikers. That shit is for ugly women who can't replace their sponsors. Me, I have them lined up around the corner so there is no point for me to stay with Kasheef."

Alija thought of what Norelle had just said and although she didn't like the girl, she had no right to judge her. *I guess it doesn't matter who I get the money from as long as I get it.*

"I'm willing to give you $75,000 if you tell the truth on the stand. All you have to do is tell what you saw and Kasheef will go away for at least twenty years," Norelle stated.

Alija looked at the clock on the nightstand. It was ten o'clock and Carmen still hadn't gotten back with her. She figured Norelle's $75,000 offer would be a good backup plan just in case her other deal fell through.

"Let me think about it for a couple days and I'll let you know," Alija replied.

Norelle wrote down her cell phone number on a piece of paper and handed it to Alija. "Call me when you decide," she said and then walked out of the room.

Alija looked at the number and rolled her eyes as she tossed it onto the dresser. She wasn't comfortable with Norelle knowing where to find her, but she didn't have a lot of money to relocate to a different motel and going home was definitely out of the question. She picked up the phone and dialed the office.

"Hi this is room nine. I'm having some issues with the heater. It's blowing out cold air. Can I get transferred to the room next door?" she asked. She'd rather be safe than sorry. She had to stay one step ahead of the game.

Chapter Nine

"Williams let's go! You made bail," the corrections officer yelled as he opened up Kasheef's cell. Kasheef couldn't jump up fast enough. He knew that he would be able to count on Stick. He was his protégé and was confident that Stick's allegiance to him would not fade just because he was locked up. He checked out of the prison, not even stopping to get his belongings because he didn't want to stay inside the musty walls a moment longer than he had to.

"She—ef!" Stick shouted as he extended his hand and embraced him quickly in one swift motion.

"Good looking out fam," Kasheef replied. "You know I got you as soon as we hit New Yitty I'mma hit you with some cash and bless you with a little something for coming through for your boy."

Kasheef and Stick made the trip back from Rikers as Jay-Z pumped loudly from Stick's custom subwoofers. Both men nodded their heads simultaneously to the beat of the music and Kasheef rolled down the windows to reintroduce the fresh air to his deprived lungs.

"Nigga it's colder than a mu'fucka outside and you got the windows down!" Stick complained.

Kasheef smiled and said, "Yo', this might be one of the last times I get to smell air outside of the gates, nah mean?"

"Yeah I feel you fam," Stick replied. "So it's not looking good for you? That little slick bitch decided to snitch huh?"

"Yeah fam. I just wish you could've handled that little job for me before she got the chance to talk to anybody," Kasheef mentioned.

Stick shook his head. "Yo', the way that chick got herself out of that was crazy. She walked right past us and into the arms of the cops, nah mean? But it's crazy though cuz she ain't snitch us out, so I was hoping she wouldn't have snitched you out and just kept her mouth closed."

"I don't know. I think I kind of forced her to talk by sending y'all at her," Kasheef admitted, remembering the message that Carmen had given on behalf of Alija.

"It's a shame too, cuz shorty had a fat ass," Stick said while licking his lips. "I would have loved to get up in that."

Kasheef laughed and replied, "You wild lil' man."

The long car ride back to New York gave Kasheef time to clear his head. He was livid with Norelle but he knew he had to approach the situation with her very carefully. She knew too much about him and the way he moved. He had introduced her to the streets and she was well aware of how he made his money. Whatever revenge he sought on her, it had to a surprise. If she knew he was out and gunning for her then she would try to hit him first and there was a good chance that her blow may hurt worse than his. He also couldn't draw any attention to himself right now. Any negative publicity would hurt his case so he couldn't take the risk of harming her physically. As they entered the city limits Stick looked over at him and asked. "Are you going to the crib?"

Kasheef shook his head and replied, "Nah, I don't want Norelle to know I'm out yet. Ride by there though so I can peep something."

As they approached the Long Island apartment community where Norelle resided Kasheef noticed a brand new Lexus sitting in Norelle's assigned car port. Kasheef smirked and nodded his head as he took in the gleaming black paint of the luxury coupe. *At least the bitch has good taste. I trained her well,* he thought. If Kasheef had been any other man Norelle's deception may have hurt, but Kasheef never let a woman get too

close to his heart. It was one of the many reasons
he'd never told Norelle that he loved her. He
felt that he could only love something that was
unflawed and since no human could ever be perfect he knew that to love someone would only be
setting himself up for disappointment. His pride
was wounded and his ego bruised, but his heart
was intact. No tears, no lumps in the throat, or
sharp pains in his stomach . . . his emotional
state was unfazed. He would still however make
sure that Norelle got what was coming to her.
He'd make sure of it. His ego would not allow
him let it go. "Yo', you tryna make some quick
paper?" he asked.

"You know I'm about my paper fam; whatever
it is I'm with it," Stick replied.

"It's nothing big. Just tail her for a couple
days. I need to know what she's doing," Kasheef
said curiously as he eyed the bedroom window of
Norelle's place.

Stick replied, "Done."

Kasheef had Stick take him to a stash house that
no one knew about. On the outside it looked to be
abandoned, but the inside was modern and plush.
It was one of several locations where he kept loose
money. His major cash was secure in untrace-
able accounts, but he had hundreds of thousands
of dollars that had not yet been washed just lay-

ing around the city of New York. He pulled out $250,000 of dirty money. He reimbursed Stick for the bail money and gave him an extra ten stacks just because. He then had Stick drop him off at a car dealership where he quickly dropped $50,000 on a Lincoln Navigator. He then swept the mall for some fresh gear, some personal essentials, and a cell phone. At the end of the night, he checked into the Marriott in Midtown on Lexington and Fifty-first Street. As soon as he walked into the room he removed his clothes and hopped into the shower. He put his hands on the wall in front of him as he dropped his head and let the water caress his body. It had been almost a month since his arrest and he hadn't showered comfortably in a while. He had never been to jail before this and now that he had been given a taste of what it was like he never wanted to go back. His freedom was something that he had taken for granted and if he was given a second chance he decided that he was going to utilize it by getting out of the dope game. Kasheef had been so accustomed to making fast money that he never got to enjoy it. His life had been a constant paper chase ever since he was a young boy and it took for him to get locked up to realize that it was not how he wanted to live his life. He wanted to enjoy each and everyday as if he would not see another sunrise. He needed to allow himself to feel again. The streets had hardened him and now he thought it was time for a change. He figured that he might open up a few businesses to give back a little bit of all that he had taken away by flooding the streets with heroine for so many years. He was only twenty-nine years old, but he was fourteen years strong in the game. Beginning his career as a hustler at age fifteen he was seasoned and skilled at what he did. Over the years he'd accumulated more than enough money to sit back and enjoy life. *All you've got to do is get through this trial.* He closed his eyes and flashes of what happened the night of Ahmad's murder graced his brain. He could see it clear as day. It was like someone had pressed play to a movie—only this movie wasn't scripted—it was a true story. He could've tried the self defense angle, but that would have been admitting that he'd actually killed a man and he didn't think that a jury would be able to get past that fact, especially for a man like himself. Kasheef sighed and washed his body, staying underneath the stream of water until it turned cold. He thought of Alija and how afraid she had been the night of Ahmad's death. He remembered how her body had shivered violently and he shook his head as he recalled how he had let her go home that night when all along he had known he should have killed her. *I've got to talk to her,* he thought to himself. *If she is serious about*

changing her statement, I'll cash her out tonight.
He picked up his phone and dialed Carmen's number. He had to find out where Alija was staying.

"Hello?" Carmen answered, her voice filled with a husky sleep.

"Carmen, I didn't mean to wake you," Kasheef said as he glanced at the clock. It was a little past midnight.

"Kasheef?" she asked as she sat straight up in her bed.

"Yeah it's me. I posted bail earlier today. Look I need the address where I can find Alija," he said.

"Kasheef listen to me. I don't think it's wise that you go there. If anything happens to her you'll be the first person the police will—"

Kasheef cut her off. "I'm not going to do anything stupid, but I have to talk to her. I need to hear her proposition for myself." He heard silence fill the space between the phones. "Come on Carmen. I need this. This is my life ma."

A reluctant sigh filled the phone and Carmen closed her eyes. She knew what might happen if she gave away the information, but the sound of desperation in Kasheef's voice broke her down. She only hoped and prayed that Kasheef didn't do anything stupid. "Okay," she finally relented. "Okay, Kasheef. If you get caught or if anything happens to that girl, you didn't get her information from me."

"What information?" he asked, letting Carmen know he understood.

"She's at the Motel 6 in Long Island, room nine."

Kasheef hung up the phone and grabbed his keys and rushed out of the room. He had some unsettled business to handle.

"Nahla? Baby, what's wrong?" Alija asked as she held her daughter and walked around the room trying to calm her down. Her daughter had been crying all day and she was beginning to worry. What started out as whimpers of discomfort were now screams of pain and Alija couldn't get Nahla to quiet down. "You can't be hungry," Alija said sincerely. "I just fed you." She checked Nahla's diaper. "And you're not wet."

Whaaa!
Whaaa!

The crying was so loud that Alija's eyes began to tear up in fear that something was seriously wrong with her daughter. She pulled out a thermometer from her daughter's diaper bag and checked her temperature. "A hundred degrees?" Alija said in confusion. She put her hand to her baby's forehead and sure enough Nahla was on fire. "Okay La-La," Alija cooed calling her daughter by her nickname. "Okay . . . we are going to get help right now," she promised as she slipped her daughter into her winter wear. She didn't even place her in her car seat, instead she held her daughter against her chest and grabbed the seat with her other hand as she headed out the door.

Whaaa! The crying was continuing to intensify. "I know sweetheart . . . I know. Mommy's going to make sure everything is okay, don't cry." She ran to her car and strapped her daughter inside. She was moving so fast that her hands were shaking. She slammed the back door and ran around to the driver's door and hopped in, but when she went to turn her car over it wouldn't start. "No! Not right now! Please start!" she yelled as she hit her steering wheel. After trying for ten minutes straight she decided to call an ambulance. She couldn't just let her daughter suffer, especially when she didn't know what was wrong. She jumped out of the car and grabbed Nahla out of the back seat.

Whaaa!

A car pulled up behind her as she fumbled to unlock her motel room and balance Nahla all at the same time.

Whaaa!

"Alija!" she heard a male voice call. She turned around and stared into the face of death himself...at least to the man who had tried to bring death to her and her child.

Whaaa!

"No!" she screamed as she began to bump her motel room door with her shoulder. She finally got the door open and rushed into the room, but before she could close it Kasheef had muscled his way inside the room.

Whaaa!

"Please . . . please don't hurt me! I won't . . ."

As soon as Kasheef saw the look in Alija's eyes he instantly felt guilty. He could feel the fear radiating from her body. Her hands were shaking so violently that he was sure she would drop her child.

Whaaa!

"Shh! Shh!" Alija whispered in her baby's ear as she backed away from Kasheef, putting the bed between them. "Please don't—"

Kasheef put his hands up. "Calm down ma. I didn't come here to hurt you," he said in his most convincing voice.

Whaaa!

"Oh God Nahla!" Alija cried. She was afraid for her life.

"Listen to me," Kasheef yelled in frustration. "I didn't come here to hurt you Alija. I just want to talk."

Whaaa!

"Yo', she doesn't sound good. Why is she screaming like that?" Kasheef asked.

Alija was reluctant to answer, but figured that if Kasheef had come to kill her that she would already be dead. "I . . . I don't know. She's been crying all day and she's running a temp. I was about to take her to the hospital, but my car . . . it won't start."

Kasheef approached Alija with his hands still raised in front of him for her comfort. "Give her here," he said as he took the baby from Alija's arms.

"No! Please—" Alija begged as she reached for her daughter.

"Look, get her shit together! I'm not about to do shit to you girl! I'll drive you to a hospital," he stated firmly with authority.

Whaaa!

Alija nodded and grabbed the diaper bag. She went to her car and pulled out the car seat to transfer it to Kasheef's Navigator. Kasheef placed the child inside. "Get in," he told Alija.

She did as she was told and Kasheef pulled off, burning rubber as he hit his gas in flight of the emergency room. Alija was silent and couldn't believe that she was inside of Kasheef's car. She still didn't trust him, but he was her only hope of getting Nahla some help. When they arrived at the hospital she jumped out and rushed her daughter inside.

"Help me! Please! There is something wrong with my baby," she told the nurse sitting behind the desk.

The nurse looked down at Nahla and by this time her face had a bluish tint to it. "What's wrong with her?" Alija asked.

"Give her to me . . . we'll take care of her," the nurse said as she tried to pry the little body from Alija.

"No, I want to go with her," Alija cried.

Kasheef came up behind Alija and pulled her away. "Let them do their job ma," he whispered in her ear. She let go and cried as she watched them put her baby on a stretcher and wheel her through the emergency doors.

"She has lead poisoning and pneumonia?" Alija asked in disbelief as she sat beside her daughter's tiny bed in the hospital. "How? I mean how did she get it?"

The doctor nodded and replied, "If she's been in an environment where there is old paint on the walls. Maybe a daycare, or restaurant, even your own home may have some old layers of poisonous lead-based paint on the walls it can affect her immune system. She is young so her lungs are not as resistant to infection as an adult's would be. Fluid can build up easily in an unsafe environment, especially in an area that is infected with lead."

"But she's going to be okay, right?" Alija asked.

"Yes. After a little bit of time, she is going to be fine. It is a good thing you brought her in when you did. If she'd gone over night with that much lead in her blood she may have died. Just hearing those words made Alija cry out in pain. She couldn't imagine life without her daughter and she had to take a minute to gain her composure.

"I'm sorry," she said as she wiped her nose with a tissue the doctor offered.

"It's quite all right Ms. Bell. We'll keep Nahla for a couple weeks so that we can rejuvenate her lungs and immune system, but she will be perfectly healthy after that," the doctor said. "We do, however, need for you to fill out your insurance information so that we can bill the company for her treatment."

"I don't have any—" before Alija could finish her sentence, Kasheef who had been standing near the doorway interjected.

"We'll pay cash."

"Okay then, the accountant at the front desk will take care of you," the doctor said. "I'll give you both a minute with your daughter, but visiting hours are over. You can't stay long."

Alija nodded and the doctor exited the room. Alija looked at her daughter and stroked her tiny hand. "Thank you Kasheef. If it wasn't for you—" she whispered without looking his way.

"You're welcome," he replied, interrupting her. They both stayed in the room for another half an hour before the hospital staff came in to put them out. As promised, Kasheef paid Nahla's medical bills and then escorted Alija out of the building. When they were inside his truck he said, "I didn't come to hurt you tonight."

"Why did you send those dudes to my house to kill me?" she asked. "I wasn't going to say anything. I only went to the police after I felt my life was in danger."

"I apologize," he said as he drove through the city streets. "I was being selfish, trying to save my own neck."

"My daughter was in the house that night Kasheef! I'll do anything to protect her," she said.

"I know. I realize that," he responded.

"How did she get lead poisoning?" Alija asked herself aloud.

"Probably that fucking rat hole you living out of," Kasheef commented.

"I was hiding out from you. It was all I could afford," she replied smartly as she rolled her eyes. She noticed that they were driving away from Long Island. She began to panic and without hesitation she punched Kasheef in the side of his face.

"Aghh!" he bellowed as his hand went up to his right eye and his truck swerved. Alija kept swinging, until he pulled over the car and reached over to restrain her. "What the fuck is wrong with you girl?" he asked.

"Where are you taking me?" she asked. "You're trying to kill me!"

"Girl, ain't nobody trying to kill your ass," he replied as he flipped up his sun visor and looked into the mirror at his damaged eye.

"Then where are we going?" she asked breathing hard as she looked at him suspiciously.

"I was taking you to a better hotel. I didn't want you to have to take your little girl back to the same place where she got sick," he said.

"Oh," she said, feeling stupid.

"Yeah *oh* mu'fucka," he chastised. He shook his head and looked in his car mirror at his throbbing eye. "Sit ya' ass back," he said as he smirked at her. "I said I'm not going to hurt you."

She did as she was told and calmed down while he completed their drive. They pulled up to the same hotel where he was staying. He purchased another room and they rode the elevator to the twentieth floor. Alija reluctantly followed him inside the room and he handed her the key.

"Make yourself at home. You can stay as long as you'd like. It's on my credit card so they'll just keep charging it until you check out," he explained.

She looked around the luxury room and was grateful that he had checked her into a better environment. The 700 thread count sheets and marble bathroom floors were a drastic change from the likes of Motel 6. "What did you come to my motel for? I thought you were still locked up," she said as she sat down at the table.

"I posted bail today. My lawyer came to see me about the offer you made. I wanted to talk to you about that," he said. "Are you really willing to go through with it?"

"Look, I don't want you to think I'm some money hungry hood rat, but I've got to look out for my daughter. She means everything to me and you took what little security I had in my life away from me. If you pay me the money, I'll get up there and say that you are not the man who killed Ahmad," she promised.

Kasheef stared at the girl and was reminded of how magnetic she had seemed the first night he had met her. The same night he'd shot Ahmad. "Okay," he said.

"Okay?" she looked up in surprise.

"I'll pay you the money. I'm not trying to go to prison for the rest of my life. I know you saw what went down. It was either him or me, so I don't regret what I did. I am sorry you had to witness it though," Kasheef said. "And I'm sorry about sending them niggas in your crib." His words were sincere in his apology because he meant everything he said. He made his way to the door. "I'll drop off the first half of the money tomorrow morning. You'll get the other half after you take the stand. I'm in 2106 if you need to get with me."

Alija nodded and smiled graciously as she walked him to the door. "Thank you Kasheef . . . for not killing me I mean," she joked.

"Thank you," he replied with a smirk as he pointed to the tiny black bruise she'd left near his eye. "For the black eye."

She closed the door behind him and a sense of relief washed over her body. She slid her back down the door until her bottom reached the floor. "Thank God," she whispered. "Now all I have to do is make it through this trial."

Chapter Ten

Alija slept comfortably in the lavish hotel room and when the sun peeked through the curtains she didn't want to get up. It was the most rest she had gotten in a while and her body thanked her graciously for the change in atmosphere. The luxurious concierge room was significantly grander than the motel she had been hiding out in. She stretched her body as she yawned and slowly arose from the bed. Opening the curtains, she looked down onto the busy New York streets beneath her as sunlight streamed into her room. It was amazing to her how her life could be in shambles, yet everything in the world still ticked on normally as if she was not hanging onto her sanity by a thread. She wondered if any of the people below her could possibly have a life as complicated as her own. A knock at the door startled her and she turned to the intruding sound in annoyance. *It's only 8:00 . . . why is housekeeping knocking this early?* She thought as she went to answer it. She pulled the door open, ready to cuss somebody out, but to her surprise, Kasheef stood fully dressed and dapper as ever in hood gear.

"Good morning," he greeted warmly as he invited himself into the room. She pulled the hotel robe tightly around her frame and ran her fingers through her hair uncomfortably as he stared at her.

"What are you doing here? I . . . I mean it's so early," she stammered.

Another knock at the door frightened her and she looked at Kasheef in fear. She did not know what to expect from him yet and the way he had sent a hit squad for her the first time she certainly would not put anything past him.

"You've really got to stop looking at me like that," he said as if he were offended. "You make me feel like the boogeyman or some shit." He opened the door and in walked the concierge with a huge platter of food in his hand. He sat it on the table and Kasheef tipped him generously before he made his exit.

"I thought you might be hungry," he said as he sat down and pulled some of the plates in front of him.

"Hold on one second . . . I'm just going to freshen up," she said as she tip toed to the bathroom. Staring at herself in the bathroom mirror she frowned at her disheveled appearance. *I can't believe I was standing in front of him looking so crazy,* she thought. She washed her face, brushed her teeth, and pulled her hair up in a loose ponytail. When she exited the bathroom she gasped at the sight in front of her. Her hand shot up to her mouth in shock.

"$100,000." Kasheef spoke calmly as if that amount of money were chump change. The smug demeanor that he possessed was as if he were born amongst riches. It was obvious that he was accustomed to the finer things in life. He had spread the money all over Alija's bed and laughed as she stood there stunned beyond belief. It was the most money she had ever seen in her entire life. The hundred dollar bills wrapped in bundles were breathtaking. It was the most beautiful thing she had ever seen. She could not pick her jaw up from the floor.

"I um . . . wow. Thank you," she whispered sincerely. That type of money could change her life. She had always been a girl form the hood. She had never aspired to be anything else, but the money in front of her could elevate her status and help her provide a new life; a new perspective for her family.

"Don't thank me. You are going to work for this cash ma. You're about to make me look like a saint. I want you on the witness stand saying that I'm feeding starving kids in Africa," he said.

Alija laughed and Kasheef motioned toward the food. "Let's eat. You can tell me how you're going to spend my money."

Alija smirked at him but she answered his indirect question. "I'm going to take care of Nahla and get as far away from New York as I can. I just don't feel safe here anymore," she admitted. "You know how the hood views snitches."

"You don't have to worry about all that. You don't have to leave New York. I'll put it in the streets that you're good people," Kasheef stated.

"Thanks but no thanks," she replied without hesitation. "I just need a new start. A new city for me and my baby. She is my everything."

"Where will you go?" he asked. "There ain't no better city than New York."

"Whatever you say," Alija answered sarcastically as she raised her brow in disagreement. "I'm going to Atlanta or somewhere south where I won't have to look over my shoulder every second of every day. It's slow and safe down there. I love my daughter and I don't want her to grow up here in the middle of the hood like I did." Alija smiled as she thought of her daughter growing up in a better place. "Nahla is my world."

"I can tell," Kasheef replied with a genuine smile.

"You got any kids?" she asked as she dug into Kasheef's pancakes. "You didn't order me none of these," she complained.

Kasheef laughed as he looked at the beautiful woman sitting across from him. As his eyes scanned her he could not help but notice how attractive Alija was. She was the last person he expected to be cordial with, but now that he had met her formally, he was glad that he'd failed in his attempt to get her killed. He respected her. She was a good mother and a gorgeous young woman. His eyes discreetly roamed her toned arms and ample breasts that were easily visible through the satin camisole she was wearing. Her wide hips were complimented by a flat stomach, thick juicy thighs, and defined legs. He looked down at her feet, even those were pretty. He felt like he was looking at a piece of art, her body was so well sculpted. "My fault ma. Here you can have these," he offered as he passed her the plate. "And nah I don't have kids. I haven't met anyone worth having them with. Most of these bitches out here don't need to be raising any kids anyway."

"Bitches?" she repeated in offense. She hated when niggas referred to women as bitches. It was so disrespectful and she did not doubt that Kasheef had come across many scandalous women, some of which probably were hos or bitches but she felt like the lady a man chose showed who he really was. It takes a bitch to know a bitch and a lot of bitch ass niggas were choosing women that weren't shit because they themselves weren't shit.

"Yeah ma, I'm not gon' hold my tongue. Most of these women out here are dirty," he stated as he thought of how Norelle had crossed him.

"I don't want you to take offense, but maybe you need to ask yourself why you keep attracting these dirty ass *bitches*. Maybe it's something about your dick that keeps these *hos,* coming around. I assure you that every woman ain't like that. Just the ones you fuck with," she defended as Kasheef reached into her plate to grab another bite of her pancakes.

He chuckled at her logic and replied, "You've got a point."

She passed him the plate back. "I'll share," she said. She looked at him and frowned as she remembered the visit she'd received from his girlfriend.

"What's with the look?" he asked. "You still don't trust me? You think I poisoned your food ma?"

"No, it's not that. I have something to tell you," she said. He put down his fork and leaned back in his chair, ready to listen. She took a deep breath and continued. "I met your girlfriend."

"My girlfriend?"

"Yes, some girl named Norelle came to see me yesterday at the motel. She's grimy Kasheef. She wants you to go away," Alija admitted.

"What did she say?" he asked. She knew that her words had struck a nerve because she could see his jaw clench as he grit his teeth.

"She offered to pay me $75,000 if I testified against you."

Kasheef shook his head. He couldn't believe that he had been sharing his bed with a woman like Norelle. He knew that she had deserted him and stolen his money while he was locked up, but to use his own money to pay off his witness was the ultimate betrayal.

"Take the money," he told her.

"What?"

"Take it. Tell her you're going to testify against me and take her cash. You can keep it. Use it for your daughter. When you get on the stand do what we planned. Tell them I wasn't there. I'll take care of Norelle. She won't bother you," he assured.

"Are you going to hurt her?" Alija asked. "Because if you are I don't want no part of that. I have enough on my mind. I don't need to be feeling bad over a girl I don't even know."

"Did I hurt you?" he replied.

She shook her head, not really knowing if she believed him or not. They finished their breakfast in silence and when they were done he reluctantly left, wishing that he could spend his entire day in her company. She was cool people and he enjoyed being around her. He almost felt like he had to make something up to her, make her life a little bit better since he was the one who had ruined it in the first place.

Alija walked into the District Attorney's office. She could not wait until this was over and her life returned to normal. She wished that she could get out of testifying all together, but there was no way that the state was going to let this case slip through their fingers willingly. Last night she had seen a side of Kasheef that she did not know existed. He was a hustler and she did not think men like him had hearts, but he had proven her wrong and shown her that there was more to him than what met the eye. Oddly she felt an allegiance to him. It was like they had become friends overnight. This trial had given them something in common; a bond between them that only they could understand. She had gone from fearing him to understanding him in only a few hours. Alija knew that she would have to be careful when dealing with him. His personality was magnetic while his charm was seasoned and unpredictable. She did not want to get caught up in his world. She could not afford to. She had to force herself to remember that they were not friends.

"Hello Alija," the DA greeted.

"Hi . . . I don't mean to be rude or rush this process but I really need to make this quick. My daughter is in the hospital and I need to be with her," Alija stated.

Nancy Schwartz smiled understandingly. "Alija, I completely understand. This case is so open and shut I can prosecute that murdering, drug dealing bastard in my sleep. I really wanted to know how you were doing. We can't afford to let the defense trip you up. They'll try to distort your words, twist what you say, and make it seem as if you are un-sure. Also try to stay away from any reporters who try to speak with you. We don't need our star wit-ness saying something that could jeopardize this case. If the public gets a hold of false information it could be the death of my case. I have seen many cases go awry from people talking too much. Save all of your testimony for the court. If you are okay with your testimony, and if you stick to what you told me and the police before, this entire process will run smoothly okay?" The DA was almost 100 percent positive that she was going to win this case. She was confident in her ability. She didn't think that God himself could change Kasheef's fate. She was going to make sure that he never saw the light of day again.

Alija nodded her head, "okay." Alija left the office and headed straight toward the hospital. She couldn't wait to hold her daughter. She was $100,000 richer and she could take care of Nahla. She was capable of giving her daughter the type of life she deserved, the life that she herself had never had.

She walked into her daughter's hospital room and was surprised to see pink balloons and yellow flowers throughout. She walked over to one of the bouquets and plucked the attached card.

> *To Baby Nala and Mom,*
> *Hopefully these flowers will brighten up your day.*
> *I hope you both feel much better today.*
> *You are very lucky to have one another.*
>
>   *–Kasheef*

***

Alija smiled because of the misspelling of her daughter's name, but knew that it was the thought that counted. She put the card back the same way that she found it. She was appreciative of Kasheef's gesture and a tear slipped down her cheek as she thought of what she was about to do. *Just get through this. Not much longer before all of this is over,* she thought as she went to her daughter's side. "Hey mama!" she greeted as she picked Nahla up. Her daughter reacted to her voice and opened up her eyes, but she was saddened to see that she was still very weak. The monitors that were hooked to her tiny frame broke Alija's heart. Her temperature was still elevated, but she knew that it would take awhile for Nahla to fully recover. "Well, let's see what mommy brought to entertain us today," Alija said. She reached into her diaper bag and pulled out a children's book. "*The Cat in the Hat,*" she began. She opened up to page one and began to read aloud.

Kasheef didn't want to disrupt Alija as she read the book to her daughter. He was supposed to meet with Carmen today to go over his case, but after having the flowers and balloons sent to Nahla's room he wanted to go check on her personally.

The gentleness that Alija used with her daughter intrigued Kasheef. It was as if Alija only lived for Nahla. Their love was unlike anything he had ever encountered. Now that there was a possibility for him to go to prison, he desperately wished that he'd opened up his life to more affection. He was beginning to see that the only thing that had been missing in his life was what Alija had—pure love. He stood with his arms folded against his white polo crew shirt, until Alija was done with the story. It was crazy. She was the star witness against him, but he wanted to start a friendship with her all the same. He knew that everything would be ruined if they were seen together, but he was willing to risk it. He was just as infatuated with baby Nahla as he was with her mother. He had never seen such a beautiful little girl. Seeing a mother and daughter like the one before him made him want a set of his own. In his eyes a wife and child were the perfect accessories if you could find the perfect woman, but perfection was elusive and he was not willing to settle for less which is why he had yet to find his life partner. He cleared his throat to announce his presence and Alija turned around in surprise.

"What are you doing here?" she asked sweetly.

"I just came by to check on Nahla," he said.

She stood up and placed her hands on her hips as if she was angry. "I can't believe you!"

"What?" he asked. *Yo', she be flippin' out on a nigga like she's my chick,* he thought as he touched his bruised eye gently and smiled slightly while shaking his head.

"You've known me for an entire day," she said as she got up and grabbed the card and pushed it into his chest, "and you don't know how to spell my daughter's name!"

She laughed when she saw the dumbfounded look on his face.

"Oh, you're trying to be funny," he said with a sexy smirk. "Keep ya' day job ma."

She laughed and returned to Nahla's side. "No seriously, thank you for the flowers and every-thing. She needs as much love as she can get."

"You don't have to thank me. I feel somewhat responsible, running you out of your home and all. How's she doing?" he asked.

"She still has a fever, but I think she'll be fine. The doctor said it will take a couple weeks for her to recover so I'm just putting it in God's hands," she replied.

"God? You trust *Him* that much?" Kasheef asked.

"You know what? I don't know. Before all this happened, I didn't think twice about God. I've never even been to church. It just feels like He's the only hope that I have left," she replied.

"That's cool. I don't have faith in nobody but me. Trusting other people will get you fucked up," Kasheef said.

Nahla began to squirm and whimper so Alija gently picked her up, making sure not to unplug any of the wiring. "You want to hold her?" she asked.

"Nah, I don't want to hurt her."

"Boy sit down," Alija said playfully as she stood up so that Kasheef could take her place in the chair. She placed Nahla in his arms and when her daughter stopped whining her mouth dropped in an *O* of surprise. "Wow, she likes you."

"She's so damn small," Kasheef stated as he counted ten tiny toes and fingers.

Alija laughed at his ruggedness. Kasheef reminded her of someone she used to know. Her father had died when she was a small child and the one thing she remembered about him was the way that he looked at her. He didn't look at her, he looked through her. He could tell if she was happy or sad, just by staring into her eyes. Her father could make the worst day better and he always made her smile. He was able to right any wrong, and fix anything that may have been broken; including her heart if it was ever shattered. Kasheef had the same gentleness about him. It was hidden underneath years of a rough visage, but she knew that it was there; beneath the skin. Inside his heart Kasheef was just like her father. They were built alike and she smiled at the distant memory.

"She's beautiful Alija," he whispered gently as he stared at the little girl.

"Thank you," she replied.

Staring at the little girl was causing his insides to feel strange. Nahla's skin was soft as silk, her presence as cleansing as a confession, and her eyes as penetrating as a bullet. Holding the small child in his arms was the most innocent and trusting interaction that Kasheef had ever had. Baby Nahla was tugging at his heart. He had never seen anyone so precious and he knew that after his name was vindicated the first thing he was going to do was settle down and find the woman who could bring him the same joy that he felt right now. "Contact Norelle," he said as he stared at the child in his arms. "Get the money for your daughter. She deserves the best." With those words he handed Nahla back to her mother then stood up and made his exit.

Chapter Eleven

"Dawn, can you get Kasheef Williams on the line for me?" Carmen asked then released her intercom button.

A couple minutes passed and then her phone line lit up. She picked up the call and said, "Kasheef! Why haven't you called me? What happened that night?" she asked eagerly, wanting to make sure Kasheef was not at risk for another murder charge.

"We're cool," Kasheef answered. "I've already paid her half of the money. She's game. I'm walking away from this . . . no bruises, no scratches."

"Okay, make sure you keep this quiet and stay away from Ms. Bell. She's still the enemy," she reminded him before hanging up.

Her hair upswept in a bun, she sat behind her desk with her legs crossed professionally at the ankle and tucked behind her. She inhaled deeply and let it out slowly to relax her mind. She was more at ease now that Kasheef had made the

deal happen with the witness. She was still curious about Alija's background however. Jumping
into an arrangement like this was like having
sex. She needed to know who she was getting in
bed with and it bothered her that she knew absolutely nothing about Alija. She hit her intercom.

"Yes, Carmen?" Dawn answered.

"Can you come in here please?" she asked.

A couple of minutes later Dawn entered the
room.

"What have you found out about my Alija Bell?"
Carmen asked as she removed her glasses and put
them on top of her desk.

"Not a whole lot really," Dawn replied.

"Ooookay," Carmen said. "Be more specific."

"She has no record of criminal history. She's
on government assistance and has one daughter. The birth certificate at the hospital was not
signed by the child's father so that's a dead end.
I tried to dig into her past and find out about
her family, but I haven't had much luck on that
either. It seems like I'm digging for a needle in a
haystack. It would be much easier if I knew what
I was looking for," Dawn admitted.

"I don't even know what I'm looking for," Carmen said.

"Do you think she's lying about witnessing the
crime?" Dawn asked. She knew that she was not

supposed to ask this, but the trial had garnered so much media attention that she could not help but to find out the facts first hand.

"Are you asking this off the record?" Carmen asked. She gave Dawn a skeptical look. She should not even have entertained the question, but the trial was driving her crazy and having someone to talk to about it was like a release.

"Of course," Dawn replied. "It doesn't seem like she is lying. She was there and she sounds pretty sure of what she thinks she saw. I just don't like surprises you know?"

"Well I'll keep digging boss. If I find something that's even remotely suspicious I'll run it by you and you can decide where you want to take it from there," Dawn suggested.

"Thanks Dawn," Carmen said. "You're the best."

When Norelle received the phone call from Alija informing her that she was willing to deal with her, she was ecstatic. With that one conversation, Alija erased all worries from Norelle's heart. She sat in the parking lot of Motel 6 and waited for Alija to arrive. She hated this part of town and couldn't wait to pay Alija so that she could high tail it back to her fabulous life in the city. Checking her rearview and side mirrors continuously, she just felt like she would be robbed at any minute. After today she would be home free. She planned on going to celebrate that night. There was no way anyone could talk her out of going to enjoy her riches and freedom. *Kasheef can rot his ass in the jail cell for all I care,* she thought. It was time for her to find a new man. It was out with the arrested baller and in with the new, upcoming hood star. She was indeed a hustler's wife. It didn't matter to her which hustler it happened to be as long as his money was long and his name rang bells in the streets. Norelle was relieved when she noticed Alija pull up behind her. She got out of the car and walked around to the passenger side of Norelle's car. She tapped on the window. Norelle unlocked her car doors so that Alija could hop in.

"Thanks for showing up," Norelle said.

"No, thank you for showing up," Alija replied. "Do you have the money?"

"So what are you going to say on the stand?" Norelle asked as she pointed to the oversized Gucci bag in the backseat.

"I'm going to tell the truth. I was there that night. I saw everything and when I get on the stand everyone in the room will feel as if they were there too. I may even shed a few tears," Alija laughed.

"A'ight girl. Thanks for looking out. You know we women have to stick together," Norelle said.

"Like magnets," Alija answered. She unzipped the designer purse and saw stacks of money. "Is it all here?"

"Yeah it's there," Norelle stated.

Alija opened the door and walked back to her vehicle. Once she was inside she watched Norelle drive away. "Stupid, stupid bitch," she mumbled as she tossed the money in her backseat and headed back to the Marriott. She was feeling real thick. She now had $175,000 in her possession— all cash. She still had more coming in once she testified. Feeling nostalgic and unable to contain herself, she palmed her cell phone from the table and called her sister.

"Mick, I need you to start working on that jury. Opening statements are tomorrow morning. Plant that seed early so that nothing goes wrong. At the end of the trial I'm going to break you off a'ight?" she said.

"You know I got it on my end. Keep in touch," Mickie replied.

"I will, but not too much. There is so much riding on this. Let's not get sloppy. We don't want to get caught," she reminded her sister. "Just stick to the plan."

***

"Yo', Sheef, Norelle just left Motel 6," Stick reported as he tailed her two car lengths behind.

"What she been doing?" Kasheef asked.

"Nothing really, spending up all your dough like crazy. I've been seeing her around that nigga Fiasco," Stick reported.

Kasheef felt his blood boil at the mention of Fiasco's name. He was a new cat who had come into New York from the Midwest a couple months back. He had come around shaking things up since Kasheef's arrest because he knew that Kasheef could not make a move of retaliation because it would draw attention to his case. Norelle was getting out of pocket by messing with his adversary and he wanted to smack the taste out of her mouth for breaking the code.

"Fiasco, huh?" Kasheef seethed anger through every word as he grit his teeth. He wasn't bothered by the fact that Norelle was messing with another man. He was hot because of the way that she went about it. She was disrespectful and was now associating with the enemy. "What else is she doing?"

"She just gave ol' girl a big ass purse though."

"Okay, stay on her. I'mma let her see my face tonight. See what she got to say for herself, nah mean?"

"She gon' shit a ton of bricks," Stick shouted with laughter in his voice. He would have paid to see the look on her face. "You want me to handle her since you under so much heat?"

"Nah, fam. I got something else planned for her. That's love though baby. Good looking out," Kasheef responded.

"Get at me when she's on her way to the crib later on tonight. I need to know when to show up," Kasheef said.

"One." Stick disconnected the call with a twisted smile on his face.

Norelle couldn't contain herself. She had dropped off the money and now her future was secure and her fate was in her own hands. With a safe full of money, she felt accomplished. It didn't matter to her that she had swindled her way to the top. She called Carmen and asked if she wanted to meet her for drinks. They decided to meet at the 40/40 in Manhattan. Norelle stayed dressed to impress so there was no need for her to stop and change. She was slowly becoming a diva and socialite—all on Kasheef's expense. She walked into the club with a newfound independence. Since Kasheef had gone away she did feel lonely, but she knew that money was harder to attain then men so she felt that the switch was worth it. Kasheef was easily

replaceable, money was not. As she sat down at
the bar she noticed Carmen walk through the
door. Stepping into the popular club wearing
a crème Fendi pencil skirt and ruffled blouse,
Carmen was dressed just right for the occa-
sion. Her fashionable appearance fit right into
the upscale atmosphere of the club. Hood fellas and businessmen alike, who were working
with major chips all turned their heads to get
a peek at Carmen's backside as she sashayed
by. Norelle smiled as Carmen approached and
they kissed each other once on each cheek before taking their seats. Norelle had just become
reacquainted with Carmen so she decided to
keep her recent actions concealed from her.
She didn't know how she would react and she
definitely didn't want Kasheef to find out. With
Carmen being Kasheef's lawyer she knew that it
would be a conflict of interest. She also did not
need Carmen to pass judgment on her. Norelle
knew what she was doing was wrong, but to her
it was worth it. She did not need random opinions of people trying to tell her how to live. She
was going to do her regardless—right or wrong.

"Hey!" Norelle shouted over the loud music.

"How have you been holding up?" Carmen
asked.

"I'm good. Real good actually, but can you
do me a favor and not talk about Sheef's case

tonight. I just need a break from it all," Norelle insisted.

Carmen nodded, "I understand."

Stick entered the club and spotted Norelle sitting at the bar next to Kasheef's lawyer. He walked to the bar, knowing that Norelle would never recognize him. Kasheef kept his women separated from his friends. They were the treasure that everybody wanted, but no other man could get too. Kasheef was smart, he never gave another man the opportunity to get in his woman's ear and now Stick was glad that they had never met. He took a seat directly next to the two women and ordered a drink from the bartender. He pretended to blend in with the crowd as he listened to the conversation going on next to him.

"I bought a new place," Norelle said.

"Really? Where?"

"It's in the city, in a building near Union Square. I just need a change. It doesn't feel right sleeping in my old place. The police turned it upside down and it just doesn't feel like home anymore. I had furniture delivered there today. I just want to forget about the past and move forward," Norelle said making up a small white lie. "As a matter of fact, I think I may sleep there tonight."

Stick pulled out his cell phone and sent a text message to Kasheef.

Ya' girl bought a place near Union Square. She's going there tonight. I'll tail her to find out the exact address.

Kasheef received the text message and knew exactly where Stick was referring to. He did not need Stick to tell him where it was located. Norelle had shown him the vacant condo a couple months ago and he had been considering buying it as a birthday gift for her. He shook his head in contempt and headed toward his destination. Norelle was showing an entirely different side of herself. He had known that she had her faults, but she had turned out to be a complete snake. When he arrived he looked up toward the luxury building as he parked his car across the street. He knew that Norelle would be shocked to see him and he was well aware of the temptation he had to break her neck. He urged himself to remain calm. He had to do this right. What he had in store for Norelle was much worse than death. He just had to be patient.

Norelle stumbled into the elevator. She was a bit tipsy from all of the cocktails she had consumed while at the club. It was the first night that she would spend at her new apartment and the first thing she wanted to do was peel out of her clothes and enjoy her Jacuzzi style bath tub. She opened the door and stepped into the apartment. Darkness and unfamiliarity enveloped her and she ran her hands along the walls as she searched for a light switch. When she finally found one, the high ceilings and hardwood floors were illuminated. She walked down the narrow hallway and into the living room and gasped when she saw a male figure sitting on her brand new furniture.

"Who are you? What are you doing in my house?" she asked. The man didn't respond. "I'm calling the police." Norelle ran toward her door, but stopped mid step when the man spoke.

"I didn't know you were buying a new crib," Kasheef said slowly . . . calmly.

Norelle ran and turned on the light in the living room. "Kasheef?" she asked. Her nerves got the best of her and she began to stutter. "Wwh . . . when did you get out? Wwh . . . why didn't you call me to let me know you were home?" she asked nervously as she backed up toward the front door. She knew that she was caught. Here she was buying condos and cars while she was telling her man that she didn't have the money to bail him out. She was busted, now all she could do is run for her life.

Kasheef stood up and walked over to Norelle. "You planned on leaving me?"

Norelle opened her mouth to explain, but no words came out.

"Huh?" Kasheef asked in a whisper. His low tone was almost more menacing then his yell and the look in his eyes sent shivers up Norelle's spine. "You were just gon' leave me in there?" He approached her and until her back was against a wall. He put his hands around her neck and rubbed gently as he stared her in her eyes.

She closed her eyes and flinched from the unexpected.

"You afraid of me now?" he asked.

She nodded truthfully, but didn't open her eyes. She saw her life flash in front of her. She couldn't understand it. *How the hell did he get out without me knowing about it?* She wondered. *Why didn't Carmen say anything?* Kasheef's face was inches away from her own. He was so close to her that she could smell the peppermint scent of his breath. "I'm sorry," she stammered.

"I know why you did what you did," he said as he backed away from her.

Confused is the only way to describe what Norelle was feeling. She was speechless.

"Please come sit down with me and talk," Kasheef said as he took a seat on her plush leather sofa and patted the cushion next to him.

Reluctantly, Norelle obliged and sat down near him, being sure to leave a bit of space between them just in case he decided to pounce on her.

"All of this is my fault," he continued. "I know what type of woman you are Norelle. I know you better than you know yourself. You are high maintenance. You live to be on top. Everything that I've provided you with over the years you deserved. I knew when I met you that you were not attracted to me. You were attracted to what I could give you. What I could do for you, nah mean?"

"That's not true," Norelle whispered back, attempting to keep up her facade.

"You ain't got to lie to me ma. I know your game and I respect it. You had your use for me. It was the money. I provided you with a lifestyle. Me, I also had my use for you. You were my trophy. You were the woman I stepped out with when I wanted to shine," he said as he lifted Norelle's chin from her chest with his finger. She smiled slightly, but was still unsure.

"So, you're not mad at me? Because I swear Sheef I'll pay you back every dime," she promised quickly. "I just didn't know what to do. I never thought you would go to jail."

"I'm not gon' lie to you; when you first left me stinking up at Rikers I was hot. That shit had me tight, but it's not important anymore. I'm out and I understand. See, even though we were using each other, something happened to me while I was with you. You stole my heart ma," he whispered smoothly. "So even if I go away, I still want to make sure you're straight. I know you were just worried about you. You didn't know how you were going to survive, but I'll never leave you stuck like that. I want you to be okay and financially set even if I go away," Kasheef explained.

"I don't know what to say Sheef," Norelle replied. "I just wish you had told me before I did all of this. Now you will never trust me again." Norelle really didn't have any remorse for what she had done, but she was for damn sure going to play this new role he had assigned her. The way he was talking he was going to make sure she was okay for the rest of her life and she was going to cooperate in order to get more money. *I slipped up this time,* she thought. *But once Alija testifies, the jury will find him guilty. When I'm sure he's in jail for life I'll drop him like hot grease.*

"Let's not worry about that," Kasheef stated. "I just want to enjoy the little bit of time that I have left with you. Just in case I lose in court, I want to make each moment count."

Norelle hugged Kasheef in complete disbelief at how naive he was. *I would have been hustling his ass if I knew it was going to be this easy,* she thought. Kasheef gripped her waist tightly and then pulled away from her and said, "Look before I go in, I'm going to hit you off with a lot of money. Don't keep it in the house. Stick up kids gon' automatically assume that I left you with my stash so it won't be safe to keep it here. Tomorrow morning I want you to go and open up a bank account. I'll make sure you have something to put in there a'ight?"

"Okay Sheef," she replied as she took his face in her hands. "I love you."

"I know you do." Kasheef hugged her and frowned. He found it funny how the words *I love you* could slip out of her mouth so easily. It was because of women like her that he did not believe in love. Women like Norelle, made it hard for him to believe that love really existed because they lied on love's behalf so easily as if it meant nothing. He pulled away and headed for the door. "I've got to go."

"Wait!" she yelled. "Why won't you just stay here?"

"I don't want you to be involved in any of this drama. The first day of my trial begins tomorrow. You'll be better off if we keep our distance.

I'll come and check on you though. Call me after
you open the account. I'll have the money for you
in a couple days," he said.

Norelle blew him a kiss and Kasheef left without responding. It had taken all that he had not
to choke the air out of Norelle's lungs. He was
just happy that he had not lost his top. Revenge
was so much sweeter when it was unexpected.

Chapter Twelve

"Hello ladies and gentlemen of the jury. Over the course of this trial the defense is going to use a barrage of illusions to trick you into freeing a guilty man," Nancy Schwartz began her opening statement while leaning on the jury box and pointing one finger toward Kasheef. "They will hold no punches as they try to paint a lovely portrait on a dilapidated, cold, brick wall. They may even try to bring up the past of a little boy raised in an urban environment who had no choice but to adapt to his surroundings. Let me put this question in your mind before all of this even begins. What does any of that have to do with a murder? Upbringing, charity contributions, or any other tool that the defense tries to use has nothing to do with murder. They are just distractions. Good distractions I might add. As a matter of fact, let's give a preemptive round of applause to the defense right now for their creativity." Nancy Schwartz walked straight over to the defense table and stood directly in front of Kasheef. She clapped her hands loudly before turning her attention back to the jury. "You see ladies and gentlemen, Ms. Rose here is a skilled magician who has made many charges disappear for many known criminals."

Carmen smirked, but did not interrupt. She knew that the DA would be pulling out all stops in trying this case. This was Carmen's first big case and the DA was trying to make it seem like Carmen had defended John Gotti or something. Nancy Schwartz was declaring war on Kasheef and she wanted to first, draw blood. She wanted to be inside of the heads of the jurors, but she would have to do much better if she wanted to intimidate Carmen. Carmen tapped her pen against the desk and listened on.

"Don't let her turn this trial into another one of her magic shows. Over the next couple weeks, the state will present you with the facts. We will give you an eye witness account of what occurred on the night of March 21, 2008. A courageous young woman, who can identify the killer of Ahmad Simmons, has agreed to share with you her account of what happened that night. There can only be one person to blame and the state will prove that person to be Kasheef Williams. Mr. Williams is the one responsible for the murder.

It is his fault that a little girl will grow up without a father. It is his fault that a mother had to bury her son. It was at his hands that this tragic murder took place and now it is in your hands to bring him to justice. It is your responsibility to right this wrong." District Attorney Schwartz gave Kasheef a smug look before she took her seat. Kasheef shifted uncomfortably in his chair.

He leaned over to Carmen, "Who the fuck is she looking at like that?"

Carmen grabbed his arm and squeezed it gently. "Don't worry about it. I got this."

Kasheef turned around and scanned the crowd. Norelle sat directly behind him as if it were her place to be by his side. He gazed past her when he noticed Alija sitting in the last row of the room. He winked his eye and saw her smile, then turned back around.

It was Carmen's turn to deliver her opening statement and she was a woman determined as she approached the jury looking fly as ever. Her long, tailored, tan Dolce pencil skirt, a high rise design, stopped right below her bust line. She wore a silk tan blouse with a ruffled neckline and a sleeveless tan vest to accent her outfit. Her Giuseppe stiletto pumps click clacked against the floor as she walked.

"Hello ladies and gentleman of the jury, how are you all doing today?" she asked with a genuine smile. She decided to take the laid back approach with her jury of mostly women. She quickly scanned the faces of the jury. Two white women, five black women, one Hispanic woman, three white men, and one black man could either make or break her entire career. All that she had worked hard for was riding on this.

"I am here to set the record straight. Mr. Kasheef Williams is not a criminal, nor is he a threat to our society. In fact, the DA is right. He has contributed thousands of dollars to local charities and even political figures. In fact, I believe Mr. Williams contributed $50,000 to Judge Martin's campaign when he was up for judicial election." Carmen turned toward the judge who turned beet red at the public revelation. Several members of the jury chuckled and Carmen continued. "He's never been in trouble a day of his life. It seems to me like he would work his way up to something as big as murder!" she said incredulously. "You know? Give himself a little bit of practice. Maybe commit a couple robberies, get himself an aggravated assault charge . . . something. Murderers are not made overnight," she argued. "Kasheef Williams is a law abiding citizen who does not have the stealth or the malice in him to commit a crime of this magnitude. He's had no practice. No priors whatsoever. He is simply the wrong man and while the state is here wasting your tax dollars the real killer is roaming free around our city streets. The district attorney can call me a magician and try to put all of these biases into your heads to help her case, but the truth is I represent the underdogs. I speak for those who can not speak up for themselves; the men and women who would otherwise be trampled on and punished for crimes that they were not responsible for. All I'm asking you is to keep an open mind while you are hearing this case. Don't let the state make your decision for you. This is someone's future you are playing with. Be 100 percent sure that the man before you is your murderer. If you feel like he's the perpetrator of this crime then by all means, convict him. If you have even the slightest sliver of doubt that leads you to believe that something just doesn't quite add up then you are obligated by law to let my client go. None of my so-called magic is needed here. The only thing I need from you ladies and gentleman is an open mind. An open mind is all you need to render a fair and just verdict. I can assure you that Mr. Williams is innocent. Now I just have to get you all to see the innocence in this man that I see."

The first day of the trial went by quickly. Both sides went through the coroner's report of the body. The short man that sat on the stand gave a very detailed account of the decomposition of Ahmad's body once it was recovered from the river. The prosecution used gory details to horrify the jurors and played the sympathy card by reminding them of the family that Ahmad had left behind. Carmen could tell that Kasheef was concerned about the affect that the coroner was having on the jury because his body was tense and his usually calm demeanor was now anxious as he tapped his foot against the floor.

When it was time for cross examination Carmen arose from her seat and walked over to the coroner. "Was there any evidence left on the body that would indicate that Ahmad Simmons contributed to his own death?" Carmen asked.

"Well there was a small trace of gun powder on the deceased's hands," the coroner replied.

"So the victim was not as heroic and innocent as the prosecution is making him out to be. There are no gun permits registered in Ahmad Simmons' name. So it may be safe to say that the shooter, whoever he may be, could have been protecting him or herself from the deceased," Carmen said.

"That is very possible," the coroner replied.

"No further questions your Honor," Carmen said and then returned to the defense table.

Both sides went back and forth for a few hours before court ended for the day. Kasheef exhausted and more worried then ever, retired to his hotel room for the remainder of the day. He lay in bed with his hands behind his head. He thought of his trial as he felt the stress build in his shoulders. He couldn't ask for a better lawyer. Carmen was great and was doing a damned good job, but there was only so much that she could do. The prosecution had it out for him. They portrayed him to be this horrible monster and he could see their words taking its toll on the jury already. They wanted a bad guy and Kasheef was it. A small knock at the door interrupted his thoughts and he walked somberly over to it. When he opened it up, Alija stood before him in a black BCBG jogging suit that hugged every curve on her voluptuous body.

"Hi," she said in a low voice. "I just came to check on you. I could tell by the look on your face that you weren't happy in there today. I thought you could use a friend." Alija smiled half-heartedly as she looked up at Kasheef.

Kasheef moved to the side to let her in, but peeked his head into the hallway to be sure no one had seen her come to his room.

"Don't worry, I made sure I was low key," she said, knowing that they were not supposed to be associating with each other. "Now what was wrong today? Tell me what's on your mind."

"They are trying to put the noose around my neck."

"Why are you so worried?" she asked. "You have the entire thing in the palm of your hands."

"I know but when I'm sitting in that courtroom I feel like I'm choking," he admitted. Being vulnerable in front of other people was something that Kasheef did not do often. He was surprised that he was opening up to Alija in the way that he was. "How's lil' mama doing?"

"She's good. I went to see her after I left the courthouse. She's still not ready to come home yet though."

He walked over to sit down on his bed. With his face buried in his hands he sighed deeply. Alija was shocked at this new connection she felt with Kasheef. He was her enemy, but here she was in his room. She was beginning to view him as one of the only friends she had. One of the only people who could understand what she was going through. *If he only knew,* she thought regretfully. She sat down next to him. "Everything will be fine. We just have to get through this. Once this is over we can go our separate ways," she said.

"What if I don't want that?" he asked as he turned his head to look at her.

Tears filled her eyes and she willed them away, but didn't respond. She wrapped her arms around herself as if she were cold. "I don't think you know what you want Kasheef. Not long ago you wanted me dead . . . now you're saying you want me here with you? I think you're just alone right now and you think that I'm what you are looking for. You just found out all that stuff about your girlfriend and you are searching for a quick replacement; someone who you can trust. Or maybe you just want to play with my head and get involved with me because of our agreement. I don't know what is up with you, but if you think I am who you want or what you want in a woman. Believe me, I'm not. You have no idea who I am. You don't know anything about my past or what I'm capable of. I will be nothing but heartbreak for you."

"I've been alone my entire life ma. I just see something in you. When I look at you, I respect you and I have never felt that way about anyone. I can kick it with you, nah mean? I see you with your daughter and it just feels right. It all feels right when I'm with you," he admitted.

"But it would be so wrong," Alija whispered as she touched Kasheef's face with her hand. If it had been under different circumstances, she may have given him a chance, but the way that their paths had crossed would forever haunt her. She just could not take it there. She could not allow herself to. "I have to be honest with you. You scare me. Just the way that we met and—"

Kasheef cut her off, "I would never hurt you."

"My heart seems to know that. I mean for these past few days you have been the only person I can talk to, but my mind . . . my mind is telling me that not too long ago, you wanted me dead. What if I had not gotten away from your goons that night?" she asked as she stared into his face. "I would be dead and quite possibly my daughter would be dead."

The way Kasheef looked at her as she spoke caused her to blush. He stared at her so intensely that she had to break his gaze. He intimidated her. "That was then," Kasheef whispered as he brought his face toward hers. She pulled away, he pulled her back . . . taking control of her, commanding her to come nearer until their lips touched. He kissed her slowly. "Now I'll kill anybody who tries to bring harm to you," he said as he gently sucked her bottom lip into his mouth. Alija resisted, putting her hands up against his chest and pushing him away. "No, this isn't right . . . you're not for me," she whispered, but the softness of Kasheef's full lips drew her back in each time she pulled away. "I'm sorry ma," he said to her repeatedly as he kissed her smoothly; his voice like a classic melody to her ears as she gave into him with regret. "I'm sorry . . . I need you. Don't tell me no."

Aljia's heart raced as she returned his kisses passionately, their tongues intertwining like a slow dance. "Kasheef," she moaned knowing that she should stop. This was not apart of her plan. He was getting to her and he was a completely different person than what she had first expected.

"Shh!" he said as he pulled her shirt over her head. His kisses trailed from her mouth to her neck to her hard dark pearls as he moved from one breast to the other, circling her erect nipples with his tongue as he palmed them softly.

Alija's back arched and Kasheef stood then picked her up. She wrapped her legs around his waist and the womanly crease between her legs was soaked in anticipation. Kasheef's hands massaged her round behind and his fingertips melted into her skin causing a wave of pleasure to pulsate through her body. He put her on her feet and reached down between her legs. When he brought his fingers out they were dripping wet. "Do you want me to stop?" he asked.

"Yes," she said as she backpedaled toward the door. Kasheef watched her walk away and as she opened the door he came up behind her and closed it, pinning his body against hers.

"Don't leave ma," he whispered in her ear as he planted kisses on the back of her neck. She closed her eyes, her hand still on the door handle. "Make love to me ma."

"No," she answered softly, her eyes closing as she felt his hands on her body.

"Stay," he coaxed.

"No," she moaned as she felt his hand palm her soaking love box through her jeans. It felt so good that her breath got caught in her throat.

"Yes," he whispered as he turned her around, looking her in her steamy bedroom eyes. "Say yes."

"No," she whispered as she reignited their kiss.

Kasheef removed her pants and picked her up by her behind, her legs wrapping around him again.

"Say yes for daddy," he commanded.

"Yes," she finally moaned. He lay her down on the bed, where she spread her legs and invited him into her warmth. He filled her up with ease. Her walls contracted against the width and size of his manhood. Her fingernails dug into his back as their bodies moved in unison to an inaudible beat. Kasheef rolled into her gently and she matched him thrust for thrust. He admired her while he sexed her body. He had never had a sexual experience like the one he was having right now. His emotions were attached to his actions. He felt something for Alija and because he had never loved another person in his life he could not say that love was what he was feeling. He just knew that it was different. It was better. He kissed her nose, her forehead, her collarbone, anyplace that his eyes graced his lips followed. She was perfect. Every inch of her body, of her soul, of her heart was perfect. It wasn't that she was without flaws, but he was blind to them. She had a few stretch marks here and there just like every other chick in America, and her attitude could match that of a lioness, but to him these things were flawless. He did not want to change a single thing about her. To another man she may not be the total package, but Kasheef was finally realizing that when you find the one person that was built for you, you are blind to their imperfections. Alija was the perfection and companionship that he had been searching for his entire life. The same way that he had fallen in love with her baby daughter while she was sick in the hospital; he was falling in love with Alija who was now beneath him in his bed. Their passion intensified as a slow grind became a fast pace as their carnal passion took control. Kasheef felt the tension building up in his toes and when she moaned, "Kasheef I'm cumming."

"Me too ma, me too," he whispered as he plunged in and out of her honey pot while she dug her nails deep into his muscular behind. "Ooh shit," he whispered. Alija had to have the best pussy ever. He closed his eyes and slowed down while going in as deep as his tool would take him.

"Kasheef!" she moaned as her body shuddered. He felt her warm womanly fluids break through her dam and flood onto his shaft. The feeling was so incredible. It was so warm and wet that he reached his peak and came with her.

Exhaustion wreaked her body and Alija inhaled deeply as she tried to catch her breath. She could not believe what she had just done. The heat of the moment had taken her life in a direction she had never anticipated. She could feel a tear slide down her cheek and Kasheef wiped it away while looking her into her eyes. They were deep with emotion and he felt as if he could stare at her forever.

He opened his mouth to speak, but Alija silenced him with her finger. She shook her head and said, "Don't. Don't say anything to ruin the moment. Just hold me. We've only known each other for a few days . . . so this can't be real . . . so please don't say anything. Just be here in this moment." Kasheef couldn't stop staring into her eyes. He felt lost and in her eyes he found the path that he should take. He lay down and brought her into his arms. Just being in the same room with Alija was like playing with fire. If the state knew that the two had been in contact, they would charge him with witness intimidation and no matter what Alija said on the stand, people would think he coerced her testimony. Kasheef could feel the rise and fall of her chest as she breathed deeply. The rhythm of her heartbeat was soothing to his damaged soul. He didn't know what she was thinking or what would become of them, but he did know that he cared for the woman lying in his arms and if he had his way he would never let her go.

Daylight came peeking through the curtains of the hotel and Alija stirred from her peaceful slumber. She was still wrapped in Kasheef's arms and she reluctantly slid from underneath him. *What am I doing?* She thought frantically. *I'm not supposed to catch feelings for this man. Where are my clothes?* She found her belongings folded neatly and placed inside one of the drawers of the armoire. She tip toed as quietly as she could around the room and slipped into her outfit from the night before. Finding a pen and paper on the night stand she left Kasheef a note.

I can't do this with you. I wish that I could, because no man has ever made my body feel the way that you did last night, but it is not right. I know that you don't understand, but just trust me. Everyone involved would just end up getting hurt.

She didn't sign her name and left the note on the vacant pillow in Kasheef's bed. She kicked herself all the way to her room. Now she would have to keep her distance from Kasheef. She had to admit that it was hard to deny his charm. There was a swagger about him that lured her in. Every time she was around him she felt jittery, like a school girl who had a huge crush but she couldn't fall in love—not with Kasheef. She picked up her cell phone and dialed Mickie's number. Her sister answered on the first ring.

"Where have you been?" Mickie asked. "I came by the motel to make sure everything was alright and you weren't there!"

"I checked out of the motel. I'm in a hotel in Midtown," Alija explained.

"Midtown?" Mickie questioned. "Bitch where did you get Midtown money from?"

"Never mind all that. You're not supposed to be coming to see me Mick! Don't fuck this up!" Alija yelled the words as she sobbed into the phone. She was overwhelmed and she just needed her life back.

"Whoa! What the hell is wrong with you?" Mickie asked, sensing distress in her sister's voice.

"Nothing Mick. I'm sorry. I'm just tired of all of this, you know?" she asked. "I called you to tell you to make sure the jury was still on track. You don't have any individuals trying to have their own opinions do you?"

Mick smacked her lips and replied, "Girl since when have I ever given anybody the option to have their own damn point of view. I got this. Unless you tell me differently, the jury is going to do what I say."

"Okay good. After this is over we are all going to be a lot richer. Kasheef is going to pay me the money after I testify," Alija said. "So just hold on Mick."

"A'ight girl. I love you."

"Love you too," Alija answered and then hung up the phone.

Kasheef read the note and crumbled it in his hands. He was aware of the fear that he had instilled inside Alija, but he was positive that he could erase the negative connotations that she had formed in her mind regarding him. She needed time, but that was something that he was not guaranteed. He had to have her now. Kasheef arose from the bed and showered quickly. Court was due to reconvene in a few hours and he had some business he needed to handle before he met up with Carmen. Clad in formal Sean John apparel, the black suit and Steve Madden shoes distinguished him. At six foot three, he hung a suit quite well. He went to visit his accountant who managed his money and made sure that it was kept securely overseas. He wanted to make sure that all of his accounts were undetected by the IRS. The last thing he needed was a tax evasion charge to add to the stresses he was already dealing with. After being sure that his money was protected he left, headed for Norelle's condo.

He knocked on the door and was greeted with a smile as Norelle pulled him into her home. "Hey you! What took you so long to come and check on me? I have been missing you," she said. Kasheef could see how he had been blind to her true intentions. Norelle was a great actress and never broke out of character. Even now she was still acting, pretending to care for him. She was indeed a beautiful liar.

"I had a couple of things that needed to be taken care of," he answered. "Come take a ride with me."

Norelle grabbed her clutch purse and followed him out of the apartment. "Where are we going?"

He put his hand on the small of her back and led her to the car. He opened the passenger side door and guided her inside. "To handle this business," he responded. "You saw how the prosecution did me yesterday. I may be going to prison and I want you to be straight. I got the money in the back seat. I'm about to take you to a bank so that you can open yourself an account and deposit it." He made sure that he was sincere in his tone. He wanted her to trust him and naively she did. *Money hungry bitch,* he thought to himself as he got in his car and pulled away from the curb. He took her to a Chase bank, pulled curbside, and said, "Go ahead."

"You're not coming in? I don't even know how much money this is," she said.

"Nah ma, I can't come in there with you. I'm under investigation so we don't want anybody to think that this is my money. You have to do this yourself so that you will have no traces to me. This is your cash now," he said as he leaned in and kissed her lips. "I just want to take care of you."

She smiled and kissed him back. "I'll be back in a minute," she said as she took the briefcase out of the backseat and headed into the bank.

I can't believe how stupid he is, she thought as she sashayed into the bank. She walked to the reception area where she was greeted by a banker.

"Hello, how can I help you?" he asked.

"Yes, I'd like to open an account," she said as she sat the briefcase down and popped it open, revealing the money that lay neatly inside. The banker's eyes opened wide and he motioned for her to come into his office. Norelle didn't hear much of what the banker explained to her. The only thing she kept thinking about was the new life she would lead once Kasheef was locked up. After giving the banker her personal information like address and social security number, they counted the money which totaled out to $400,000. She intended on putting the rest of the money that she had originally stolen from Kasheef's safe and would have more than a half million dollars. A wicked grin crossed her face as she shook hands with the eager banker. She walked back out to the car where Kasheef waited curbside with his seat leaned back and one hand propped on the steering wheel.

"You get it done?" he asked.

"Yeah it's all taken care of," she replied. She hopped into the car and he pulled away, satisfied that everything had gone off smoothly. The $400,000 was a huge chunk of what he had acquired in the streets. In all, he had two million stashed in his accounts. He had given Norelle all of the money that he had not washed yet. He still had product on the streets which had the potential to earn him more revenue, but he wouldn't be able to touch that for awhile. He planned on putting Stick onto his connect. After he beat this case he was going to retire and enjoy some of the dirty money he had made over the years.

"Are you ready?" Carmen asked.

Kasheef looked around the crowded courtroom. Cameras flashed in his eyes and spectators whispered speculative comments regarding his arrest, but he ignored it all. He was looking for someone in particular. He was hoping to see Alija in the back row, but she wasn't there. Her absence caused a dampening spirit to overcome him.

"Kasheef?" Carmen called his name to get his attention. "Is everything alright?"

"Yeah, everything's fine," he replied as he focused his attention toward the judge who was now entering the room.

"All rise!" the bailiff announced. "The Honorable Judge Campbell Martin presiding."

"Be seated," the judge said.

The day's events began with the prosecution. The District Attorney arose from her seat and one of her paralegals rolled a television stand to the middle of the room, facing it toward the jury.

"Yesterday the defense and I bantered back and forth. You heard a lot of speculation and hearsay as to what occurred the night Ahmad Simmons was shot dead. Everyone wants to know. What really happened that night? The tape that you are about to view will answer all of those questions. You will see it with your own eyes," she said. She bent down and pressed play on the VCR and the account of what actually happened came across the screen. Ahmad's face was clear as day as he held up an unidentifiable man. The other figure's face could not be seen from the angle that the camera had recorded the scene. You could make out his clothing, but no facial figures. Alija's face was clear as day as she peeked into the room. The jury sat back and watched as what had began as a robbery ended in a murder. Nancy Schwartz turned off the tape and watched the reaction that she got from the jury. They couldn't believe that all of this had been caught on candid tape and that the man who had done it was still roaming free. "The young woman that you saw in that tape is willing to tell you what she saw that day. She fingered Mr. Williams. She called him out by name for the police. How can you deny that he is not the murderer?"

Carmen stood up as she watched the DA take her seat. "That tape proves nothing," she started out. "If anything, it shows the type of person that Ahmad Simmons was. He initiated the chain of events that night. He had a gun of his own in which he used to threaten the figure in that tape. The face of the murderer is not even visible and until you hear the witness testify you should not let this tape affect your decision. It is weak evidence, circumstantial at best." Carmen walked down the aisle and toward the door of the courtroom. She opened it up and in walked ten different men. They were all the same complexion as Kasheef, the same height as him, and they all wore the same pair of designer jeans just off their waistline and the same shirt that Kasheef had worn the night of the murder. "Judging these men from the neck down, which is the only part of the shooter that can be identified, can you distinguish between them? The assailant had no identifiable scars or tattoos. Can you tell these men apart?" she asked persistently. "I can't. As a matter of fact, any one of these men can be the perpetrator." Carmen could see the question marks going off inside of the jurors' heads. That was all that she needed to do, create doubt; reasonable doubt. She turned toward the gentlemen who she had brought in and said, "Masks please." Each man placed a black hood over their heads making their faces unidentifiable and their bodies identical. "As you can see ladies and gentleman, there is no way to distinguish these men from one another without having a clear view of their face. They all look like the murderer. It could be anyone."

Kasheef couldn't help the sly grin that crossed his face. Carmen was slick. She had game and it was at that moment that he realized she was worth every single red cent that he was paying her. He was more confident than ever before. Carmen had just put a major dent in the prosecution's case. He already had Alija on his team so all he had to do was let the case play out. Kasheef barely listened for the remainder of the day. His mind kept drifting back to the night he had shared with Alija. Her smile, her eyes, her face were all embedded in his mind. He wondered why she had not shown up for his trial today. After seeing her attend the court sessions the prosecution decided that it be best if she stayed out of sight until it was her time to speak. They did not want her there until it was absolutely necessary, but silently he wished he could see her face. Just the fact that she sat in the back of the courtroom gave him reassurance. He turned once more to make sure that he had not missed her, but she was nowhere to be found. Norelle sat behind him, but only because she thought everything was good between them. She was a woman who presented herself under false pretenses. Her outward beauty was magnificent, but inward she was just as ugly as the grimiest niggas in New York. While stick up kids held men up with their guns, Norelle's weapon of choice was a combination of good looks and good pussy. Kasheef shook his head and turned back around just in time to hear the judge adjourn the trial for the day.

Kasheef stood and buttoned the top button to his coat jacket. He leaned in and kissed Carmen professionally on the cheek and whispered, "Good job today ma. Once this is over I owe you dinner a'somethin'."

"I eat lobster and steak," she replied with a smile. "Let's just hope tomorrow is just as successful. She gathered her paperwork, walked out of the courtroom and bypassed the reporters as she hopped into the Lincoln Town Car that awaited her curbside. She headed toward her office. She had a lot of reading to do on other cases. Since taking on Kasheef as a client she had been neglecting her other responsibilities in the office. She knew that it was important for the senior board members of her firm to see her as well rounded, so she needed to balance all of her case trials successfully. With Alija on their team now and the excellent cross examinations she herself was presenting, she was confident that the win was in the bag. All of her hard work was paying off. She was finally moving up the corporate ladder. It did not bother her that she was riding Kasheef's criminal wave to the top. *As long as I get there,* she thought as she cruised the city streets. *I'll be the youngest senior partner and the first black woman to achieve that at the firm,* she thought proudly. Losing was not an option, she was determined to win. By any means necessary.

Chapter Thirteen

Alija sat near her baby's side. She was well enough to be off of the monitors and Alija was relieved to finally see some progress in her daughter's health. She held Nahla on her lap as she sat in the rocking chair flipping through a photo album.

"See look," she cooed to her daughter and pointed at the pictures. "Here is you and mommy." She turned the page. "Here is you, mommy, and daddy." A smile crossed her face as the pleasant memories from the photos flooded her memory. "And here is you again . . . you are mommy's little angel Nahla." She kissed her baby lovingly. "Mommy loves you."

"Hmm, hmm." Kasheef cleared his throat to announce his presence in the doorway. Alija turned toward him.

"Oh," she said in a surprised tone. She closed the photo album and slid it into Nahla's diaper bag. With her daughter still in her arms she stood and looked at Kasheef awkwardly. "I did not know you were standing there."

"I wasn't. I just got here and I didn't want to startle you," he said. He moved closer to her and she took a step back. "I see Nahla's doing better." He held out his hands to the infant and to Alija's astonishment, Nahla leaned toward Kasheef. She handed her daughter over to him and smiled.

"You might want to stop coming around so much. She is going to think you are her father. You already have half of the nurses thinking you are her daddy," Alija joked.

"Speaking of that . . . where is her father?" Kasheef asked. He knew that Alija had a past, but he wanted to know exactly what he might be getting himself involved in if he chose to pursue her seriously after the conclusion of the trial.

"Not that it's any of your business, but he ain't in the picture anymore," Alija said with one hand on her hip.

"I was looking for you today in court," he admitted. "I was hoping you would come." Nahla playfully touched his face as he talked and he held her so intimately that someone would have thought that Nahla was his child.

Alija looked down at her feet nervously. "After last night . . . I just felt uncomfortable. I don't know. I just needed to think. Plus, the prosecution doesn't really want me there anyway. Witness intimidation, you know?"

"I intimidate you?" he asked sincerely.

"I don't know," she responded. "I just need time to think."

"About?" he asked.

"My life, the plans I have for her life," Alija said while pointing to Nahla.

"I was hoping you might make room for me in both of your lives," he said genuinely. Alija's eyes met his and he reached out his free hand to pull her near. She resisted a little, but eventually stepped toward him. He wrapped his arm around her waist and kissed the top of her head. Closing her eyes she inhaled the scent of his Hei cologne and put her hand on his chest.

"What am I doing?" she asked aloud.

"Letting me in," he replied. He looked at baby Nahla and smiled. "Ain't that right ma?"

Nahla gurgled baby sounds and Kasheef said, "See, she's feeling the kid."

Alija laughed and held onto him tightly. Just the sensation of a man's strong embrace made her feel safe. It was something that she had been missing. For a moment she had some security in her world and she desperately wanted to hold onto it. She finally noticed the gift bag that sat at his feet. "What's this?" she asked as she bent down to pick it up. She peered inside and found three Dora the Explorer children books. "Thank you," she accepted graciously.

He sat down in the rocking chair and grabbed one of the books from Alija then began to read them to Nahla. Alija watched in amazement as Kasheef interacted tenderly with her daughter. Most men would run in the other direction if she told them that she had a child, but Kasheef seemed to be running toward her. They were developing the most intimate connection she had ever had with another person in her life. She was afraid; afraid that the actions that she were taking would change her life forever. The two of them stayed by Nahla's side until she was fast asleep. After they put her back into the pediatric hospital bed, they walked out with Kasheef's arm draped around Alija's shoulders.

"Did you drive here?" he asked as they stepped onto the pavement of the parking lot.

"Nah I took a cab. My car is bullshit. One day it works, the next day it doesn't," she said.

"You gon' have to cop you something new with all that cash you extorting from me," he said jokingly. She hit him on his shoulder and smirked in response. "Get in," he said as he opened his passenger door for her and she looked around nervously.

"Kasheef, we can't be seen together," she whispered.

"We good, there ain't nobody out here. Besides my windows are tinted. Quit worrying," he assured her. She hopped into the truck and he closed her door before walking around to the driver's side.

When they pulled up to the hotel Kasheef let her out at the entrance. "I'll meet you in my room in a couple minutes," he said while slipping her a key card to his room.

She got out of the car and walked into the lobby of the hotel. She could not help, but to feel as if her life had become one of those romance movies as she peered around to make sure there were no prying eyes around her. After taking the elevator to the twenty-first floor she had to take a couple deep breaths before she made her way down the hallway to Kasheef's room. Her nerves were making her feel as if she were going on her very first date. The flutters in her stomach felt more like eagle's wings then butterflies, causing her to feel faint. When she walked into the room her eyes watered from the sight in front of her. "Oh my God," she whispered as she looked around her. There were candles and rose petals everywhere. An intimate indoor picnic for two was set up on the floor. Her heart raced. She was definitely in over her head. She was beginning to fall for Kasheef and he had made it perfectly clear how he felt for her. She didn't even realize he was in the room with her until his arms were wrapped around her waist.

"Why are you doing this?" she asked weakly as her eyes closed against her will and she enjoyed the feeling that his lips brought to her neck.

"I want you," he admitted. "I don't know what it is about you Alija, but you were built for me ma."

Alija turned to face him. "Kasheef I have a daughter. I can't just start this with you as easily as another chick could. There are things that complicate this situation. All of my decisions affect her. I'm just trying to do right by her. I know what kind of life style you lead. I saw you kill Ahmad. Why would I want my daughter to be around that? I'm not even gon' front like I've always been responsible, but that night in the club you forced me to change. Seeing him get shot right in front of me . . . that changed my life Kasheef . . . forever."

"I hear you ma, but that still ain't telling me what I need to know," he stated frankly. "I want to know if you can put all that aside. I want to take care of you and Nahla. I would never let anything happen to you."

Against her better judgment, she kissed his lips sensually. The chemistry between the two of them was insane. It literally felt like sparks were flying throughout the room and every single spot of her body was sensitive to Kasheef's touch. "You've got my heart ma," he said with his forehead pressed against hers. "I've never felt the things that I'm feeling for you."

"Where would we fit in your life Kasheef?" she asked with genuine concern and doubt.

"There's nothing but room in my world ma. It's just me. I'm all alone. I have been for a long time now. Things are going to be a little crazy until this trial is over, but after that my life . . . our life together, will go back to normal," he guaranteed.

"I don't want to live in New York," she said.

"Then you don't have to. Whatever you want Alija, I'll give it to you," he promised.

"I don't know why, but I believe you would," she replied.

Kasheef pulled her down onto the floor where he pulled out fresh fruits and wine for them to indulge in. It was the most romantic thing that any man had ever arranged for her and Alija was open. They sat up into the wee hours of the morning just talking and laughing. They got to know each other a little better. Kasheef noticed that it was five o'clock in the morning and he yawned deeply.

"Yo', I ain't stayed up talking like this since I was in middle school kicking whack game to the young girls on three-way," he stated with a chuckle.

"I know. It's easy to lose track of the time though when you're in good company like me," she bragged playfully. "You better get some sleep though. You have court in just a few hours."

"Right now that ain't important," he whispered. "The only thing that matters right now is me and you."

Alija blushed as Kasheef massaged her feet. "Why me?" she asked.

"Why you what?"

"Why are you so interested in me?" she asked more clearly.

"You remind me of someone I used to know," he replied.

She frowned. She did not like being compared to some other girl. That meant that she was only a replica of the real thing he had lost. "So you really aren't feeling me. You just like me because I remind you of some other girl you used to love. What she broke your heart and I'm her substitute?"

"You remind me of my mother . . . she passed away a couple years ago," he said.

Alija immediately felt like an idiot for assuming the worse. She pulled her feet away from his grasp and quickly apologized. "I'm sorry."

"It a'ight ma, you did not know. There is just something in you. It's in your swag, like you're strong. You are a survivor. You out here trying to raise your daughter on your own . . . it's just a combination of things that remind me of her. She raised me by herself. I never knew my father. We were like our own team. A two man show. We never had much, but we had each other and that was always enough. She was the only woman I have ever loved. I was protective of her. I would have done anything to save her. Nobody else just seemed to be able to compare," he explained.

"She sounds like a beautiful person Kasheef," Alija admitted.

"I know. After she died I didn't think about her for a long time. It just hurt too much. It was so much easier for me to just shut off my heart than to deal with losing her. Now every time I look at you, I'm reminded of her."

"Is that a good thing?" she asked. "I don't want you to hurt every time you look at me."

"Nah ma. It's the exact opposite. My heart seems to heal the more I'm around you."

"What are you saying Kasheef?" she asked as tears filled her eyes.

"I'm not trying to scare you off ma," he said. "But I care a lot about you."

"I care about you too," she replied with her head bowed in shame.

Kasheef frowned. "Why do you say it like it's a bad thing?"

"You could never understand. I don't even want to get into all of that. It's too late and I'm too tired," she said.

Kasheef pulled her body near his and grabbed the covers and pillow from the bed. He wrapped them over their bodies and within moments they were both sound asleep.

The next day Alija awoke to the sound of a baby's laughter. She thought she was dreaming, but when she opened her eyes she saw Kasheef holding her daughter.

"Say hi to your moms shorty," he said as he placed Nahla in Alija's arms. Alija looked up at him in shock.

"When did . . . how did you?" she was so stunned that she could not form any questions in her mind to ask.

"I went and talked to her doctors. They said that it was safe to bring her home. I knew you missed her and since they thought I was her father anyway they allowed me to sign her discharge papers," Kasheef explained.

"Thank you Sheef," she said, calling him by his nick name for the first time. Hearing her shorten his name let him know that she was becoming more comfortable in his presence and he smiled.

"You're welcome," he answered. "Are you coming to the courthouse today?"

"Yeah I'll be there," she replied. He fixed his tie and leaned in to kiss Alija on the lips.

"Bring baby girl too, she might be my good luck charm," he said as he walked out of the room.

The trial went on for the next couple days and Alija found herself sitting in the back row with her daughter faithfully. The District Attorney bitched a fit about her being there, but she refused to leave. She told them that she wanted to face her attacker when really she just wanted to show her support for Kasheef. After surprising her and bringing her daughter home early Kasheef had claimed a tiny piece of Alija's heart. It was too hard to deny him, so she found herself giving in slowly . . . regretfully. Kasheef was grateful for her support and was slowly but surely falling in love with this woman. They spent every day together. Alternating between his room and her room. She liked how he was so at ease with Nahla and she appreciated how he respected her as a woman, but more importantly as a mother. Alija was like a temporary vacation from life's everyday grind for Kasheef. She was who he talked to when he needed to get something off of his chest. She gave him peace of mind and her smile brightened up his day no matter how bleak it may have been. It got to the point where he honestly could not remember how he had ever been happy without a woman like her by his side. Even when they were not in each other's presence, she stayed on his mind and he carried her spirit in his heart. She was as close to perfect as someone could ever be and once the trial was over he planned on showing her how much he appreciated having her in his life.

The most important day of the trial was approaching fast. The day that Alija was expected to take the stand was only a few days away and everyone was on edge. Everything was riding on her and she knew it. She was nervous; she did not want to mess up in any way. She had to speak her words as if she were telling the truth and she figured the easiest lie was to say that Kasheef was not even at the club that night.

Kasheef still had some things to take care of. He contacted Carmen and asked her to set up a meeting with a federal prosecutor.

"Kasheef, I don't think it is wise for you to contact them in the middle of your case," she advised.

"There's just something that I need to handle, concerning the drugs that were found during my arrest," he responded.

"Kasheef I really think you should wait until they bring those charges against you," Carmen said.

"Why haven't they indicted me yet?" Kasheef asked curiously knowing that the fed boys didn't play. Going up against them, your chances were slim and he hoped to be in the wind by the time those charges came back up.

"They must be after someone bigger than you . . . maybe your supplier?" Carmen speculated. "Either way, if you go in there you are going to ruffle feathers."

"Just set up the meeting," he said before flipping his phone closed. He was eager to get this business with the feds handled. Even if he beat the murder there was a good chance that he would be convicted if he was prosecuted for the heroine charge. This is where the game got tricky for him. He had to play chess with his enemies and knock out two birds with one stone. He had to be smart in how he moved. At this point, any wrong move could land him a permanent spot behind the bricks and he dreaded that more than he dreaded his own death. Kasheef never wanted to put his life in jeopardy again and since he planned on sharing his life with Alija he knew that he would have to give up the drug game. He needed to make preparations to make a clean break so that his past could never come back to haunt him. There was still the issue of Kasheef's connect. He would not want to see Kasheef's business go. Kasheef knew that he would have to have some type of incentive to provide Osti with if he wanted to exit peacefully. Kasheef went to a pay phone and contacted Osti to set up a meeting with one of his people who was already in the states. After that was done he contacted Stick, who had been loyal to him for years.

"I need to get with you about something fam," Kasheef said.

"A'ight, come through my spot," Stick responded. "Give me about an hour."

"A'ight, I'll be there in an hour. It's important so make sure you are alone," Kasheef instructed before snapping his phone closed.

Stick was only twenty-one, but was as thorough as most old heads in the game. Kasheef had found him when he was ten years old and was selling candy to people coming out of the grocery store in the middle of the summer. The young boy had caught his attention because Kasheef knew that schools did not do fundraisers during summer vacation and he confronted the boy about it. A youthful Stick was honest and when Kasheef asked him why he was posted in front of the store, Stick replied, "I'm just trying to get my shine up like you. I'm trying to eat."

Kasheef laughed at the boy and purchased his entire stash of candy bars. He rode by the same spot for a week straight and sure enough, Stick was posted in front of the store relentlessly getting his hustle on. Kasheef respected the young boy's tenacity and grind. He immediately recognized him as good corner boy material and put Stick onto the game. Stick had moved up in the ranks quickly because he was smart and ruthless. If Kasheef was not going to be getting money anymore he knew that there was no better person to pass his empire down to then Stick. An hour and a half later Kasheef pulled up to Stick's Crown Heights project building. He placed a call to Stick to let him know he was in front of his building. A couple minutes later Stick came walking out of the building.

"What's good fam? You sounded kind of urgent on the phone," Stick said. He stepped into the car and Kasheef pulled away from the curb.

"It's about time you came into your own fam," Kasheef said as he whipped his Navigator through the hood. "I think you're ready. I've seen your ass grow up from a little hard headed mu'fucka to a

grown man. Ain't no need for you to play the back
no more. You were patient and you waited until
your time came fam. I appreciate that. Most of
these mu'fuckas out here trying to take what they
haven't earned. You have earned it though."

"Earned what? You speaking in circles," Stick
replied.

"My spot. I'm retiring from the game. After
the trial is over, I'm done. I've already set up a
meeting for you to meet with my connect and
everything," Kasheef said.

Kasheef reached out his hand and Stick shook
it. "Yo', fam, good looking out, but there's only
one problem."

"What's that?" Kasheef asked curiously.

"That new cat Fiasco is fucking up the game. I
guess he's been moving weight out of the Bronx.
He's been stepping on my toes lately. He is coming to our blocks shooting up shit, scaring our
workers. He talking bout' ain't nobody working
them corners unless they slanging for him,"
Stick replied.

"Why am I just now hearing about this?" Kasheef asked harshly. "I knew the nigga was trying
to make money and I didn't hate on that, but
now this lil' mu'fucka getting out of hand. When
niggas gon' learn to stay in they lane?" he asked
heatedly.

"I didn't want to cloud your head. You know with the trial and everything I thought I should wait to let you know, but recently this mu'fucka been doing some real disrespectful shit. He's spitting venom on your name and everything. Mad niggas been jumping ship. They trying to be on the winning team nah mean? I'mma ride with you until the end fam, but you know when people think you down they automatically count you out."

"Yeah bitch niggas always do switch sides, but your boy is far from out fam," Kasheef assured as he rubbed his neatly trimmed goatee.

"I told you before I've even seen your chick Norelle with him. At first they were real low key with it, but recently she's been riding shot gun with the nigga and everything. In the club on his arm and shit . . . just real disrespectful nah mean?" Stick said.

"You have put in a lot of work for me over the years. It's your time. Don't no new mu'fuckas run New York fam. That ain't happening. I'll take care of him, you just be ready to step into the big leagues. You're the boss now," Kasheef said.

Kasheef circled the block once more before pulling back up to Stick's building. "You got to come up and have a drink with your boy or something," Stick said. "I got to celebrate fam."

Kasheef shook his head. "Maybe another time. I've got one more loose end I need to tie up," he said. He tossed Stick a cell phone. "This is how Osti will contact you. He's the only one who has that number. I don't even know it. He will call you when he's ready for you."

Stick nodded and shook hands with Kasheef once more before Kasheef pulled off. He retired back to the hotel and found himself making his way to Alija's room. He knocked softly on her door. She answered it wearing a gold lace camisole and lace boy-cut panties to match.

"Shh!" she whispered as she opened up her door and invited him. "I just put Nahla down. She was a little cranky today but—" she stopped talking when she noticed the look on Kasheef's face. "What's wrong?" she asked.

Kasheef grabbed her arm and brought her near him. With his hand caressing the nape of her neck he kissed her slowly. "I love you."

The look on Alija's face was one of shock and panic. She did not know what to say. Here he was laying all of his cards out on the table and all she could do was stand in front of him, speechless. When her heart returned to a normal pace she took a deep breath and finally, unsurely replied, "I love you too Kasheef."

He scooped her into his arms with ease. "I swear I'm gon' give you the world ma. Just believe in me. Trust me. Be loyal to me and I will give you everything you need or want. If I can't give it to you then I'll die trying, I promise you that ma."

Alija kissed his nose and replied, "I love you Kasheef. I wasn't supposed to, but I do. I promise to give you everything that you deserve."

She got into her bed where Nahla lay peacefully. "Come lay with me," she said. Kasheef stripped down to his boxers and crawled underneath the covers. He took Nahla from the bed and laid her tiny body on his chest. Alija smiled and lay underneath his arm. "Good night Kasheef."

He kissed the top of her head. "Get some rest ma."

They both went to sleep knowing that they each held the other's future in their hands.

Chapter Fourteen

The morning of Alija's testimony came quickly, too soon for some, not fast enough for others. Kasheef and Alija moved around her hotel room silently. They both had burdensome thoughts on their mind and the air between them seemed too thick to talk. Kasheef finished dressing and grabbed his keys. There was one more thing that he had to do. Before he left he stood in front of Alija.

"How do you feel?" he asked her concerned. He could see the stress taking over her face. She was usually so vibrant and relaxed, but today her features seemed to be set in a permanent scowl.

"Nervous," she answered truthfully. "And confused."

"I don't want to put any more pressure on you," Kasheef said. "I just want to let you know that I love you. I love you more than anyone in this world and no matter what happens today, that will never change a'ight?"

Alija nodded and gave him a weak smile.

"What about Norelle? When she hears me—"

Kasheef placed a finger to Alija's lips. "Norelle is already taken care of. I got you ma, just trust me." He kissed her one last time. "I've got to go," he said. Alija nodded her head, but she could not help but feel like this was the last time she would ever see him. She felt like she was suffocating and all she wanted to do was run. Run away from her problems, run away from the confusing game that her life had become.

A half an hour later he stood in front of the federal building. He took a deep breath before stepping inside, knowing that there was a possibility that they might not let him walk back out with his freedom intact. It was a risk that he had to take. He took the elevator to the eleventh floor where the Drug Enforcement Agency was located. Confident in his Calvin Klein two piece suit, he stepped to the receptionist as if he belonged with the stride of a man on a mission. "I have information pertaining to a heroine ring here in the city. I need to speak with someone in charge," he said calmly.

In less than ten minutes flat he was sitting across from Dan Greene, the chief of the DEA. "I hear you have some information regarding some illegal activities that are going on in the city," the chief said as he stared intensely at Kasheef.

"Yes, I do."

"And why are you just volunteering this information?" he asked suspiciously.

"I know you are aware of my arrest. I am going through a very public trial right now," Kasheef stated.

"I know who you are Mr. Williams," the chief responded. He leaned back in his leather chair and put his hands behind his head as he swiveled in his chair from side to side. He squinted in suspicion and added, "The question is: what are you doing in my office?"

"I'm here to help you help me. I'm sure you are aware that when I was arrested twenty kilos of heroine were found as well. I didn't know that the drugs were in the house, but I know who they belong to," Kasheef lied.

The chief pulled out a notebook and a pen then slid it across the desk, his pale fat hand contrasting with the dark mahogany wood. "Start writing," he instructed.

In one swift motion, Kasheef tossed the pad right back at him. He sat back in his seat and folded one leg across the other. "I'm not going to do your job for you. I just have some information that will lead you in the right direction. Norelle Gibson. That's whose apartment the drugs were found in. If you watch the company she keeps you will find your source. Norelle helps him move his product up and down the East Coast. If you check her accounts you will uncover a gold mine." Kasheef stood up to leave, but turned to face the chief before exiting. "I trust that this will prevent the DEA from opening a fresh case on me?" he asked, making sure that he had dotted all of his i's and crossed his t's.

The chief nodded and replied, "If this lead pans out then you have my word."

"I need better than your word. I need that told to my lawyer," Kasheef replied as he slid Carmen's business card across the desk. The man didn't like the fact that he was bargaining with a criminal but he made the call anyway.

Once everything was in place, Kasheef went to leave.

"Oh yeah, and good luck on that murder rap. We didn't need to open a fresh case on you for the drugs. You hung yourself when you killed that kid. You blacks get off on that . . . killing one another," the chief stated sarcastically as he picked up the phone.

That's what you think, Kasheef thought with a smirk. The chief did not know it yet, but he was going to have the last laugh when it was all said and done.

***

Norelle stepped out of Fiasco's BMW and kissed him gently before walking into the courthouse. Today was the day that she would receive her emancipation. She was getting ready to hear the testimony that was sure to set her free. She walked through the crowded building eagerly, hoping to run into Alija before the day's proceedings began. She saw her being escorted out of the DA's office.

"Alija!" she called out as she maneuvered her way in and out of the crowd. Alija stopped walking and turned to see who had called her name. The DA waited and watched the interaction so that she could see who was interacting with her star witness. She did not need anyone throwing a wrench in the plan. Alija was due to testify that day and she did not want any interruptions.

"I'll be right back," Alija told Nancy Schwartz as she made her way over to Norelle, looking her up and down as she approached. She couldn't help but turn up her nose at the woman. *How stupid can she be to give up a man like Kasheef? He would have taken care of her if she had just stuck by him.*

"I just wanted to make sure our agreement was still intact," Norelle said discreetly as she stood in front of Alija.

"Everything is going to go as planned," she assured her. She turned and walked away to rejoin the DA. Butterflies filled her stomach as she was placed in a small holding room until it was time for her to enter the courtroom. The state had arranged for Nahla to be taken to a daycare so that Alija could be present in court. She took several deep breaths as she paced around the small office. She hoped that nothing went wrong. She desperately needed for things to go right. The contents of her stomach sent a wave of nausea through her body and she gasped for air. She was overwhelmed that she could not hold her breakfast. She rushed to the bathroom and barely made it as she vomited in the toilet. She heaved violently until nothing else would come up. She splashed cold water onto her face. *Calm down,* she told herself. It felt as if the room was spinning and she hoped that her nerves would settle before she was due to speak. She sat down and closed her eyes before sending a silent prayer up to God. She was going to need all the help that she could get to pull this off.

"The State of New York calls Alija Bell to the stand," the District Attorney announced. The large wooden door creaked open as Alija appeared. Kasheef's heart melted when he saw her. Her skin glowed as if she had been personally kissed by the sun and her honey brown complexion complimented the cream H&M dress she wore. A large gold belt was wrapped around her tiny waist and her feet were blessed with gold, strappy stilettos. The way that her hair was pulled up away from her face allowed Kasheef to take in all of her features. At that moment he knew exactly why he loved her so much. She was his idea of perfection. She was his love. Her heels clicked against the floor as she glided up the aisle and into the witness chair.

"Raise your right hand and place your left hand on this Bible," the bailiff instructed. Alija inhaled deeply and did as she was told. She glanced over at the jury and Mickie gave her a discreet wink of reassurance.

"Do you swear to tell the truth the entire truth, and nothing but the truth, so help you God?"

"I do," she responded.

The judge looked at her and said, "Thank you Ms. Bell, you may be seated."

Alija's breath caught in her throat as her nerves took over her. She could feel the stares penetrating her as she watched the DA approach.

"Ms. Bell can you tell us where you were and what you saw the night of March 21, 2008? Please don't leave out any detail. Take us through that night as you can recall it."

"I was at Club Blaze with some friends. I was with Ahmad Simmons having a drink at his booth," she began. She glanced at Kasheef who was staring at her intensely. His facial expression was calm. He trusted her completely to deliver her testimony just as they had rehearsed.

The DA noticed her hesitate and urged her on. "Please, continue Ms. Bell."

"I was having a couple drinks with Ahmad Simmons and the club began to let out. I was a little drunk. I had been drinking all night. All of my friends had already left the club so I got up to leave too. I was halfway to my car when I realized that I had left my purse and keys inside of the club at the table that I was sitting at. I went back in to get my stuff. The club was empty, but there was light on upstairs and I could hear voices." Alija's eyes began to water and she closed them as tears began to cascade down her face.

Norelle listened intently as she waited for Alija to identify Kasheef. She bit her nail anxiously and tapped her foot nervously. She was anxious for the trial's conclusion and could not wait to move on with her life.

Kasheef's heart broke in two as he watched Alija relive that night. The tears on her face caused knots of guilt to form in his stomach. The love that he felt for Alija was unmatched by any emotion he had ever felt before. He just wanted to protect her. He wanted to be there for Alija and Nahla. He never wanted to be the cause of her pain again. He looked over at Carmen who returned his gaze.

"Is all of this apart of the plan or is she going to turn on us?" Carmen asked in a furtive whisper.

"We don't have to worry about her," he reassured.

"Now what were these voices saying?" the DA grilled.

"I don't know," Alija responded as she opened her eyes and caught Kasheef's gaze. "I can't remember."

"You can't remember?" the DA asked as she gave Alija a look that sent chills up her spine.

"No . . . I'm sorry, I can not recall what they were saying," Alija responded.

The DA stalked over to her desk and flipped through her notes. "Okay, Ms. Bell well what did you see?"

"I walked in and I saw two men. They were yelling at one another. Ahmad had a gun, but the other guy pulled his gun as a reaction and shot Ahmad. I ran after that. I did not see what happened next."

"And is the man that you saw shoot Ahmad Simmons in the courtroom today?" The DA asked.

Alija paused before answering. She looked at the jury and stopped at Mickie who nodded her head slightly, urging her on. The courtroom was so still that you could hear the faint sound of Norelle's heel impatiently tapping against the floor. Alija felt herself gasping for air as she tried to calm herself down.

What the fuck is she doing? Norelle thought as she set her sweating palms on her skirt and rubbed feverishly in anticipation.

"No," she finally answered.

No! I know this bitch is not trying to cross me. I paid her $75,000! Norelle was livid as she stood to her feet. Before she could open her mouth to speak, the door of the courtroom opened loudly as four suited gentlemen walked in. Kasheef turned around in his seat and watched the scene play out.

"Norelle Gibson?" one of the gentlemen asked.

"Order in this courtroom!" the judge yelled as he banged his gavel and the crowd whispered in speculation.

"Yeah?" Norelle responded unsurely. "Who are you?"

"My name is Agent Greene and I'm the chief of operations for the United States Drug Enforcement Agency," he stated.

"And? What the fuck does that have to do with me?" she asked indignantly.

"You are under arrest for the distribution of heroine and tax evasion," he said as he turned her around and began to apply handcuffs to her small wrists.

"What! Wait, you are making a mistake!" she screamed.

"No, ma'am this is no mistake. Pretty girls like you make me sick. You're almost worse than the drug dealers we lock up because they get involved with that life to chase tail like you. Now you have the right to remain silent . . ." the agent continued to read Norelle her rights, but she didn't hear one word. She gave Kasheef a pleading look, but the malice that she found in his gaze told her that he had set her up. They pulled Norelle out of the courtroom kicking and screaming.

BANG! BANG!

"Order in my courtroom!" the judge yelled as he hit his gavel against his desk.

Carmen looked at Kasheef in disbelief. "Is that what you had me set a meeting up with them for?"

"Just do your job ma. If you want to represent your girl after my case is over then be my guest, but it was either her or me. The bitch tried to pay Alija to testify against me. She wanted me to get this time so that she could spend my dough. She had it coming to her," he whispered and then refocused his attention toward the front.

Carmen could not believe what had just happened. She knew that she could not help Norelle right now. She had to finish her job and represent Kasheef. She shook her head in blatant disgust at him as she mumbled, "Unbelievable."

"Believe it," he whispered back.

The judge slammed his gavel several times to regain control of the room. Once everyone was silent the trial resumed. Kasheef winked at Alija as she continued. "I don't see Ahmad's shooter in the courtroom."

A look of irritation spread all over the DA's face as she persistently continued to steer her witness back into the right direction, "But Ms. Bell did you not tell a Detective Nielson of the NYPD and I quote 'Kasheef did it. I'll testify to protect my daughter' end quote?"

"I did tell the detective that I would testify in order to protect my daughter, but he is the one who brought up Kasheef Williams' name. I had never heard of him before I was arrested. He is not the man I saw," she said confidently.

The DA walked back to her chair, her frustration and exasperation made clear when she flopped down in her chair and put her hand on the side of her face while in deep thought. This was Carmen's cue to spring into action. "Your Honor, it is obvious that the state has done everything in their power to falsely convict my client. I would like to move for immediate dismissal!"

The judge looked toward the DA. "Mrs. Schwartz, do the people have any other evidence against Kasheef Williams?"

Nancy Schwartz's face was flushed and red in anger. Holding back her emotions, she stood and replied, "Your Honor, even without Ms. Bell's testimony we have provided evidence against Mr. Williams. I think that it is only fair that we proceed with this case and let the jury decide."

The judge nodded, "I agree. The trial will continue, but we will adjourn for the day. Closing arguments will resume tomorrow after which the jury will deliver their verdict."

Alija stepped down from the witness stand and if looks could kill she would have fell dead where she stood and been circled in chalk as hard as the DA was staring. She walked out of the courtroom, relieved that her ordeal was over. She had done all that she could for Kasheef. Now all she could do was wait.

Kasheef left the courtroom with a huge smile on his face. Alija had pulled it off and her tears had only intensified the affect of the false statement she had given. He was sure that the jury had believed her. As he walked through the courthouse he felt rejuvenated and confident for the first time since the trial had begun. Alija was worth every penny he had agreed to pay her. He felt forever indebted to her. The performance she had put on was sure to get him off. He exited the courthouse and descended the steps then got inside the limo that was waiting for him curbside. He went straight to his accountant's office to retrieve the remainder of Alija's money. He could not wait to see her and share his future with her.

"Are you sure you want to do this?" His accountant asked skeptically. He had witnessed Kasheef's grind over the years and he knew how long it had taken him to accumulate his wealth. "This is a lot of money. You have worked very hard for this."

Kasheef nodded his head and replied, "I'm positive. I'm going to marry this girl. She just saved my life today. I trust her."

His accountant nodded and handed Kasheef paperwork to sign. Kasheef signed them without reservations. The accountant made him copies and put them inside of the suitcase that contained Alija's money.

Kasheef couldn't wait to see Alija. When he arrived at the hotel he went to Alija's room. Before he could even knock on the door Alija opened it with a smile on her face. "I was waiting for you," she said. He scooped her into his arms excitedly and kissed all over her face.

"Aghh!" she screamed playfully and laughed giddily as he spun her around in his arms.

"I love you girl," he told her as he set her down on her feet. "Where's Nahla?" he asked.

"She's still at the daycare. I figured I would pick her up in a couple of hours," she replied.

"Here sit down, I need to talk to you," Kasheef stated seriously as he pulled a chair out for Alija. He put the briefcase on top of the small eating table and popped it open. "Here is the rest of the money that I promised you."

Alija smiled and ran her hand over the neatly arranged bills. The amount of money was overwhelming and she had to stop herself from screaming she was so happy. Even after she paid Mickie $50,000 for all of her help she would still have more than enough money to live comfortably and give Nahla the best of everything.

Kasheef removed two pieces of paper and handed them to Alija. "Read these," he instructed.

Alija began to scan the document. "Aloud," he said gently. Alija frowned and looked up from the paperwork.

"What is this about Kasheef?" she asked.

"Just read it ma. It's important."

Alija sighed and began from the beginning. "I Kasheef Williams hereby give Alija Bell joint ownership of Cayman Island Account 5487624008630 and Swiss Account 74639957203. There is a combined amount of $2,500,000 in these accounts." Alija stopped reading the document and stared at Kasheef in disbelief. "Kasheef, I can't accept this. This is too much," she objected.

"I want you to have that Alija. I'll give you all that I have in order to keep you." Kasheef stood in front of her and got down on one knee. "I need you ma. I know this is all happening kind of fast, but I know this is right. You are right for me Alija. I love you. You are the only person that I have loved besides my mother in my entire life. Will you be my wife?" The three karat platinum princess cut ring was blinding.

Alija closed her eyes. She could not believe what was happening to her. She could not breathe and she gripped Kasheef's hand tightly. *I'm not supposed to be in love with him,* she thought frantically. She felt his hand grace her cheek and before she could come to her senses she responded, "Yes. Yes, Kasheef I will marry you."

Chapter Fifteen

Alija sat nervously in the back of the court-room as she waited for the jury to come back with a verdict. She stared at her engagement ring and her stomach filled with knots. She wished that she could have talked to Mickie before the deliberations began, but it was too late. What-ever was going to happen was already in motion. There was no turning back now.

Kasheef's heart felt as if it would explode as he sat in the federal courtroom. News cameras were littered throughout while both supporters and the opposition awaited the verdict. It was the day that he would meet his fate, the day that the rest of his days would be determined by the decision that the jury rendered. On the outside, Kasheef was calm and collected. His chocolate Armani suit rested perfectly against his dark skin and medium athletic build. With his hair cut neatly in a fresh caeser and his eyes filled with sincerity, one would never guess that the man sitting before them was a drug kingpin. Kasheef scanned the jury with his eyes and couldn't read their expressions. He didn't know what tomorrow held for him and for the first time in his life he was afraid. Prison was not an option for him. To lock him up would be equivalent to stealing his pride and he refused to live on his knees. Kasheef hoped and prayed that the verdict would be delivered in his favor, because if it wasn't he was already prepared to go out in a blaze of glory. A $10,000 cash payment to one of the assigned court officers ensured that he would have his weapon of choice, a chrome .45, taped underneath the defense table. He discreetly ran his hand along the underside of the cherry wood and felt the cold steel that was strapped securely in place. It was his insurance policy.

Kasheef was not green to the game and had been in the dope game since he was a young boy, so he knew that his day of judgment was inevitable. While many glamorized the street life, he knew the real deal and was well aware that his reign could only end in one of two ways—prison or death. He would much rather hold court in the streets for his actions, in his own environment where he would at least have a chance to survive. Sitting in a courtroom made him a sitting duck. He knew that it was very possible that the jury would convict him and that the judge would throw the book at him, sending him away for the remainder of his life. He turned and stared into the eyes of Norelle, his girlfriend, who greeted him with a wink and a sexy smirk. Cameras flashed continuously in her face, but she took it all in stride. She knew that they had recognized her face from her very public arrest that had occurred the day before. She didn't care however; she had just come to see what the verdict would be for Kasheef. From her Manolo stilettos to her Marc Jacob two-piece suit with the matching clutch, she represented all that he was. He was a miracle worker and had taken her from the gutter and put her in a throne beside his own as the queen of the streets. She held her title well, no matter the cost and indeed like royalty she commanded attention. *You didn't think I would come,* she mouthed as she discreetly stuck up her middle finger. Kasheef knew that she would be out on bail, but he was confident that the feds would have enough evidence against Norelle to convict her. He looked past her and Alija's face stuck out from the crowd. She gave him a weak smile and he nodded to acknowledge her. He couldn't show it, but his heart warmed at the simple gesture that Alija had given him. Just the simple things that she did made him happy. He was glad that he had her support.

"All rise!" the bailiff announced loudly, causing Kasheef to turn back around in his chair. "The Honorable Judge Campbell Martin presiding."

"Be seated," the judge mumbled as he took his own behind the large pedestal. "Has the jury reached a decision?"

The face of the foreman told Kasheef all that he needed to know. Kasheef gripped the steel underneath the table and took a deep breath as he prepared himself for what was about to go down.

"Yes, we have your Honor."

"And what say you?" the Judge inquired.

"We the jury . . ."

Kasheef's hand wrapped tightly around the gun and the anticipation made him sweat slightly as he closed his eyes and waited to hear if he would walk out a free man or be left in society's constraints.

"Find the defendant . . ."

His heartbeat in his ears, blocked out all sound as he watched the foreman's lips mouth the words.

Pow! Pow! Pow!

The verdict fell on deaf ears as the courtroom erupted in mayhem. Norelle grabbed one of the court officer's 9 mm pistol and fired as many shots as she could get off. With rage in her eyes and her finger around the trigger she went after Kasheef with a vengeance. "No!" Alija screamed as she ran toward the front of the room. The guards drew their weapons and surrounded Norelle.

"Get down! Now, put down the gun!" they yelled. Norelle didn't comply, but instead raised her gun to finish off Kasheef who was gasping to fill his lungs with air and squirming from the hot lead that had entered his body. It was only the bullet that pierced her heart which managed to stop Norelle's relentless, burning rage and her body instantly went limp as it fell to the ground. Her head hit the floor with a hard thud and she lie motionless next to Kasheef who writhed in agony.

Alija tried to run past the groups of people who were gathered around Kasheef, but the officers stopped her. "Move! Let me go! Don't touch me!" she yelled as she struggled to get past the crowd. "Please! I need to make sure he's okay." No matter how much she fought they would not let her through. The area was quickly secured and stretchers were brought into the room to take Kasheef and Norelle to a hospital.

Everyone was confused and stunned by Alija's reaction to Kasheef's shooting. When Kasheef reached out his hand for her and whispered,

"I love you," the press went wild. Carmen and Alija locked eyes, but Alija quickly stormed off, headed for her car.

Carmen turned toward the judge. "Your Honor, the verdict?"

The judge shook his head and replied, "The jury found him guilty."

"What?" she asked incredulously. *There has to be some type of mistake,* she thought. *Alija's testimony should have been enough to free him.* She looked around at the disheveled courtroom and the blood splattered onto the floor. She turned around and found her boss standing near the exit shaking his head. His thin lips were clamped in together and she could tell he was fuming. *My career is over,* she thought selfishly. The entire case had exploded in her face and crumbled at her feet. She walked right past him without speaking. She had to finish her job and tell her client that she had lost the case and that he would be going to prison—if he lived to see another day. She fully intended on filing an appeal, but if she had lost the first case there was no guarantee that she could win the next, and at that moment Kasheef was a loss to the state.

Chapter Sixteen

Eight weeks passed before Kasheef was able to stand before the judge for his sentencing. Alija had stayed by his side the entire time he was recuperating in the hospital and he was saddened that their time together was being cut short. She sat directly behind him with her daughter in her arms. She cooed and reached for Kasheef while tears fell freely from Alija's eyes. She had been so confused during the entire trial. Now that it was over her heart ached and she felt as if her best friend was being taken away from her. Carmen sat by Kasheef's side as they awaited the judge's decision.

"Mr. Williams," the judge began. "You have been found guilty by a jury of your peers for second degree murder. Does counsel have any recommendations for sentencing?"

"Your Honor, the state would like to request that Kasheef Williams be punished to the fullest extent that the law allows," the DA said.

"Your Honor my client has been unjustly found guilty of a crime that he did not commit. I would like to state for the record that we will be filing for an immediate appeal and I ask for the courts to show restraint on Mr. Williams in regard to his sentencing," Carmen stated.

The judge removed his glasses and said, "Mr. Williams, I hereby sentence you to no less than fifteen and no more than twenty-five years in Sing Sing Correctional Facility. You will be remanded into immediate custody."

"Kasheef?" Alija cried. "I'm so sorry Kasheef," she said as she stood to hug him. He reached for her and she held him tightly. "I'm sorry Kasheef."

"It's alright ma. What are you sorry for? You've done nothing but made my life better. Listen to me Alija," he said sternly as he blinked away tears. He knew that he had to remain strong. "I'm gon' be okay. You take that money and you look out for yourself a'ight. Come see me sometime. I love you. You're the only woman I've ever loved; remember that."

The guards came and took Kasheef away and Alija stayed inside the courtroom until she could no longer see his face. With each step that he took, a piece of her left with him and the onslaught of emotions was almost unbearable as she held onto

Nahla, the only constant in her ever-changing life. She felt like there was a revolving door where people constantly entered and exited her heart, leaving her to mend the broken pieces after they were gone. She kissed her daughter and hugged her tightly. "It's all over Nahla. It's all over."

"Williams, you have a visitor," the CO yelled as he unlocked Kasheef's cell. Kasheef stood. It had been three months since he'd been sentenced and only one person had visited him so far—Stick. He had communicated with Alija through letter only. He had asked her not to come and visit him because he did not want her to see him locked behind bars, in his weakest state, and chained like an animal. He sauntered to the visiting area, his feet shackled, and his pride wounded.

"Table four," the CO told him. Kasheef approached the table and was surprised to see Alija sitting before him. She had put on a little bit of weight, but it was all in the right places and just her presence seemed to lift a huge burden from his shoulders.

"Hello Kasheef," she said with a half smile. He could tell her spirit had been dampened by his imprisonment and the sparkle that she had when he first met her was dim. The fact that he could not be with her killed him. Alija held Nahla in her arms and Kasheef noticed that even the baby had grown tremendously in the short time that he had been absent from her life.

"I miss you ma," he said, his voice heavy with built up emotion as he put his hand against the glass that separated them.

"I miss you too Kasheef," she whispered as she matched her hand alongside his. She stared at his face, taking in every single feature. Her heart fluttered at the sight of him before her and she instantly knew how they had come to be so close. At first she couldn't understand how she had let herself fall so hard. Kasheef was a forbidden love. She experienced something with him that she had never felt before. In many ways, he was her man. Ironically, he was the only man that she had ever fully trusted. "I can't stay long. I just came to give you something." Her voice broke up as if she was ready to break down, but she quickly cleared her throat and willed her emotions away.

She handed a manila envelope to the guard who was monitoring their visit and he inspected it briefly before passing it to Kasheef. Kasheef opened the folder and pulled out the first piece of paper. It was an ultrasound picture. His eyes shot up from the photo to Alija's. He stared at her more carefully and noticed the small bulge in her stomach. She was pregnant. He closed his eyes and had to stop the tears from forming behind his lids. Alija was pregnant with his first child, his only child and here he was stuck in prison unable to give her the support that she needed. He would never be able to be apart of his baby's life. He gripped the phone tightly and took a deep breath before he opened his eyes. "You're pregnant with my seed yo'?"

Tears built in Alija's eyes when she heard the sound of his voice. He was holding back his cries, but she could hear the undeniable sadness that was threatening to pour out of him.

"I'm sorry Alija," he said sincerely.

"No, I'm sorry Kasheef," she replied as she wiped away a tear that escaped her eye. "There's more."

Kasheef removed a set of photos. He flipped through the photographs slowly, one by one. There was a picture of Alija. He smiled, knowing that this would help him make it through a lot of days. Just having an image of her face would make the time go by easier.

"You're beautiful," he complimented. He went onto the next picture, a picture of Alija and Nahla.

He loved Nahla. She was a miniature version of her mother and he silently hoped that Alija was pregnant with his son. A girl and a boy would make their family complete. He pulled out the next photograph, a picture of Alija when she was pregnant with Nahla. He flipped and it was a more recent picture of Alija. He peered closely at it. "Are you pregnant with my baby in this photo?"

She nodded and gave him a half hearted smile as he flipped to the last photo. When the image registered to his brain, he dropped the pictures onto the steel table as if they were as hot as fire. He couldn't believe his eyes. He turned the picture over to make sure he wasn't seeing things and he noticed the inscription that Alija had written on the back.

> *Kasheef,*
> *I told you from the beginning that it would be so wrong for me to love you. I don't know how I let myself fall for you, but now you know why we can never be. This is exactly what you deserve.*

He turned the picture back over, his hands shaking. He stared closely.

Alija, Nahla, and Ahmad smiled like the happy family that they were before Kasheef ruined their lives. Ahmad was Nahla's father and Alija's lover.

"You killed my baby's father Kasheef," Alija finally admitted. The tension that she had carried on her shoulders since the day Ahmad died finally lifted from her and it was as if a weight had been removed from her heart.

"What?" Kasheef asked as his eyes met hers, desperately searching for answers. He shook his head, unwilling to accept the naked truth as it had been laid out in front of him.

"We were supposed to get married and make a life together after he was released from jail," she said through her tears, her voice heavy with sorrow. "I begged him not to get back in the game but he wouldn't listen. He said that he was doing it for us, so that he could take care of his daughter. You killed Nahla's father and I had to make you pay for what you took from me; for what you took from Nahla. I didn't mean to fall in love with you. That wasn't apart of the plan. I just wanted to put you away so that my daughter and I would be safe, but you got to me. You got inside my head. You offered to take care of me and you gave me what I needed to take care of my daughter. You gave me all of your money to start a new life, and you gave me your heart. It was so tempting to take Kasheef, but I couldn't forget that it was because of you that my life was in shambles in the first place. That is why you're here. For revenge," she said as she wiped her eyes and willed herself to stop crying. "Even though I love you, you have to pay for what you did to him."

He stared up at Alija as she arose from the table. He was speechless. He watched her walk over to another girl who had been sitting in the waiting area. His eyes bugged in disbelief as he recognized the girl from his trial. She sat on his jury. *Alija set me up. All along she set me up,* he thought, as his heart dropped into his stomach. He felt sick and his eyes burned but he held back his emotions. It was hard for him to believe that everything that he had shared with her had been a lie. She had seemed so sincere. Her love had seemed so real. He had thought that they were so official. She was the closest he had ever been to true love and now he was finding out that it was all a lie. *This shit can't be true.*

"Alija!" he called for her as he stood and watched her walk away. He was not willing to let her leave just like that. He had to know more. He had to keep her in his life for as long as he possibly could. It was as if the beat of his heart was dependent on her loving him. If she stopped he was almost positive that his heart would too. He was beyond the point of self preservation. Almost from the first moment he sought her out, they had become connected. He felt it and refused to believe that it had meant nothing to her. "Alija, please don't take my baby away! Don't do this to me!"

He was conflicted. A part of him was enraged and hated her for being able to penetrate his shell. She was his weakness and he resented her for making him vulnerable. Because of her, he was susceptible to pain, but the other part of him could not possibly hate the woman who was carrying his seed; the woman who had cracked his hard exterior and gotten him to love. She was the woman whose smile could brighten his darkest hour. She was his salvation and with her love he could make it through the hell to which he had been reprimanded to. "Alija!"

Alija halted mid-step. The sound of his voice caused her to close her eyes. She took a deep breath and returned to the table. She picked up the phone.

"What Kasheef? Don't you hate me now? Haven't you had enough?" She waited for him to respond, but he was silent. She could see his broken spirit as she stared into the windows of his soul. "Huh? Why do you still want me? You can't love me now, because I hate you for doing this to me! Do you hear me? I hate you," she whispered vehemently.

"Don't say that ma," he begged, his tears finally falling from his eyes. "I can't hate you Alija. I've never loved anyone the way that I love you. You put me in here, fuck it. I killed Ahmad, but you saw what went down. You know how it happened. I'm not a murderer Alija. You know me. I was protecting myself. I did what I had to do, you know that. I love you ma. Don't take my child away from me. Don't leave me in here on stuck."

Alija was bawling as she listened to him. Her heart ached because she really had fallen for Kasheef. In another lifetime he would have been her man and possibly her husband. He would have been her king, the one she shared her hopes and dreams with, but in this lifetime they could never coexist.

Kasheef could see the wheels turning in her head. "Tell me you don't love me ma. You can't tell me that Ahmad meant more to you than me. You love me Alija. I can see that shit in your eyes," he said passionately with fire in his gaze and through clenched teeth.

Alija stared him directly in the eye. "How can I raise Nahla next to her sister or brother and tell her that you are the one who killed her father? How fair is that to her? I can't let her see me love you and think that it's okay Kasheef. It's not okay. It was wrong for me to let it go this far. It doesn't matter how I feel about you. I have to think about my children. Ahmad may not have meant more to me, but he meant more to Nahla. That's my daughter, I have to protect her." She touched her stomach and finished, "I have to take care of both of them."

"They're my shorties too ma. I'm in love with your baby girl just as much as I love you. And the one that's growing inside you *is* me Alija. That's my seed yo'. Don't do this to me," he pleaded.

"You did this to yourself," she said. "Good-bye."

All this time, Kasheef thought as he put his head in his hands in despair. *She had someone working on the jury to sway them into a guilty verdict while she worked me to sway me into giving her my cash.* He looked down at the ultrasound and let his emotions flow without restraint. A combination of feelings raced through him. Rage. Respect. Love. Hate. He felt them all for Alija at that moment. She was the woman he had fallen in love with, the one he would have given his life for without regret. *She is the mother of my child yo',* he thought numbly. His heart ached in a way that he had not felt since the death of his mother. Alija was his everything and she had just walked on his heart with her Manolo stilettos. All he had wanted was her love and loyalty, but she was in fact loyal. Loyal to her man. The only problem was that her man was Ahmad. Kasheef stood up and punched the glass with all his might, struggling to let go of some of his rage. He returned to his cell. It was the place he would call home for the next fifteen years courtesy of Alija Bell. *I guess Ahmad really did get the last laugh. The nigga reached out from the grave to get his revenge.* He taped the ultrasounds to his wall. He told himself that he would look at them everyday and ask God to bless the child that he would never get a chance to meet. The ultrasounds were the only piece of his family that he had left and he prayed that one day the emptiness he felt inside could be filled by the return of the love of his life. Until then, his fate was sealed behind the steel and concrete that made up the desolate prison. Pain is love and it was the story of his life.

Kiss Kiss Bang Bang

Prologue

I can't wait until you come home
I miss you
Don't be wild'n out in Vegas, nigga
I don't want to have to fuck a bitch up

Love always,
Six

Free smirked and shook his head when he read the text message from his girlfriend of seven years. Six had been his backbone since he was twenty years old, and they had experienced plenty of ups and downs together. Although he loved Six to his core, in the past he had hurt her more than once with his cheating ways. He was young when they had first met, and it had taken him awhile to learn how to be a good man to her, but from the first day he saw her, he knew that she would be wifey. He knew that Six wasn't making idle threats either. She had fucked up a couple chicks over him. The last time she caught him cheating, she had beaten a girl so badly that the girl was hospitalized for days. That had been over a year ago, and needless to say, no other chick in Wayne County had tried to come at Free since. Everybody knew what was up, Free was taken, and from that point on, he had been faithful. "She always thinking something," he mumbled to himself as he pulled the small velvet box that contained the two-karat engagement ring that he planned on surprising her with. Six really didn't know how much Free had grown. He was ready to make it official. He knew that no other woman could hold him down the way that Six could, and he was ready to make an honest woman out of her.

"You really gon' ask her to marry you, huh?" Big Lou asked with a skeptical look on his face.

"Yeah, man. She's getting antsy and shit. She been tripping on me lately, doubting me and all that. She keeps bringing up the past. She talking like I don't love her. She still thinks that I'm on the same ol' shit."

"Nah, fam. Six knows what's up. Y'all have been through a lot together. You would kill a nigga for her," Big Lou replied as his New York accent oozed off of every word.

"Yeah, I got a good woman. It's about time I settled down with her. I'm just trying to make her happy, man."

Big Lou cracked a smile as he shook his head from side to side.

"What, nigga?" Free asked with a look of irritation on his face. He was trying to keep it funky with Big Lou because he wanted an honest opinion regarding what he was about to do.

"I never thought I would see the day when young Alfree would be ready to settle down with one chick," Big Lou responded in disbelief.

"Don't be calling me Alfree," Free said. He hated his government name and had shortened it to Free a long time ago. He fumbled with the ring box, opening and closing it repeatedly as he felt the plane prepare for its landing. "She deserves this yo'. Those other chicks can't do shit for me."

"What about that bitch Asia? Shorty got a fat ass! You gon' give all that up? Because I'll step in and hit that since you gon' be a one-woman man now. I'll give her some of this King Kong," Big Lou stated with laughter in his voice.

Free shook his head and replied, "Man, go for what you know. She do have the goods though, but I don't love them hoes. The only one who matter is Six."

"Six is a good chick. I ain't ever met a woman like her. She a gangsta too. Congratulations, man," Big Lou stated in a genuine tone.

"Thanks," Free replied as he rested his head against the leather first-class seats. He closed his eyes and thought back to the first day that his world had been blessed by Six's presence.

Seven Years Ago in NYC

The club filled quickly as New York's elite walked through the door and prepared to celebrate New Year's Eve. Everybody who was anybody came out to bring in 2002 with Twin and his entourage. Twin was the most successful party promoter in the city, and he threw the biggest parties and invited all the boroughs. Free and Big Lou pulled up to the crowded club as they watched the line wrap around the corner.

"Damn, nigga! It's jumping in that joint," Big Lou stated as he took the safety off his automatic pistol.

"Good," Free replied as he loaded his .45-caliber pistol with a full clip. He parked his black-on-black Navigator at the side of the busy street, and both men concealed the burners in their waistlines as they exited the vehicle. They walked up to the crowded club and headed toward the front of the line as they prepared to step into the club. They had no intentions of standing in the line. Big Lou had gotten them hooked up with VIP passes, so they didn't have to wait. Partygoers complained as they watched Free and Big Lou disregard the entire line.

"Hold up, homeboy," a big bodybuilder-type bouncer said as he held his hand up to stop the two from entering the building. "Y'all see that line back there?" he asked. "Unless y'all got VIP passes, y'all gon' have to wait just like everybody else."

Big Lou pulled two orange-colored, laminated passes that had *VIP* stamped on the front.

The bouncer chuckled and said, "Those ain't gon' get you up in here. Those passes are from last night's event. They ain't even the right color."

"What? My man gave me these. What color they supposed to be?" Big Lou asked, getting heated that the bouncer was trying to chump him in front of the crowd of people gathered by the door.

"The only color that matter is green, nigga," Free interrupted as he placed a knot of hundred-dollar bills in the bouncer's hand.

"True," the bouncer replied as he lifted the red velvet rope and let them into the club without even searching them.

"I'ma kill that mu'fuckin' crackhead that sold me those damn passes," Big Lou stated as they made their way to the bar.

"Don't worry about it. It's nothing. We about to get all that cake from the door. That money coming right back to me," Free stated. Free and Big Lou sat back and enjoyed the party as they waited for the guest of honor to arrive. Free checked his cell phone and noted that it was only ten o'clock. The inside of the club was already packed and there were hundreds of people still waiting outside to get in. Free's eyes scanned the room until he found the sign displayed above the door that displayed the maximum occupancy. *This nigga is cleaning the fuck up. He charging fifty a head and this mu'fucka can hold a thousand people. That's fifty stacks. Easy money,* Free thought as he felt the cold steel that rested against his hip, ensuring that it was there if he should need to use it. Big Lou made the most of his time and entertained a group of women, but Free stayed focused, clocking each and every dollar that came into the club as he waited patiently for his plan to pop off.

"It's showtime, kid," Big Lou leaned over and whispered in Free's ear as they both watched Twin and his entourage enter.

"There go that bitch Twin fucking with. She ain't all that!" one of the girls said as they spit venom on the girl who walked in on Twin's arm.

Free and Big Lou focused their attention on the brown-skinned female that had entered the club with Twin. The silk Lela Rose minidress that she wore rested perfectly on her five feet seven inch frame, showing off her thick thighs and long legs. Her body glistened a healthy glow that matched her green eyes that were obviously contacts, but she rocked them well. Her hair flowed loosely, but was pulled to one side and stopped right above her perky breast line. She was perfect from the top of her head to the bottom of her French-manicured toes and to top it off, Twin was holding onto her waist as if her pussy was laced in gold. Envious vibes spread through the room instantly as every man wished he was in Twin's shoes, and every woman wanted to be whoever the girl was. Her name instantly became "that bitch" as girls who were normally confident became insecure in their own skin.

"Damn," was all that Free and Big Lou could say as their eyes followed the woman's ass as she stepped up the stairs that led to the VIP lounge. Any other day Free would have made it a point to step to her, but today he was on business.

"Keep your eye on the money," Free stated as he watched the door. From the bar, they had a clear view of almost every angle in the club. They could even see Twin and his entourage through the clear glass of the upstairs VIP window. Free smiled as he watched money continue to flow through the door. Once the club reached its maximum occupancy, a huge smile spread across Free's face. He checked the time again. "Ten minutes to midnight," he said to himself as he watched Twin make his way from the VIP room to the DJ booth.

"What's good, New York?" Twin asked as he took the microphone. He had a bottle of Cristal in one hand and the microphone in the other. "I want to thank all y'all mu'fuckas for coming through and bringing the New Year in right with your boy."

Free smiled as he listened to Twin's slurred speech. It was obvious that he was drunk. Twin wasn't pissy, but Free knew that he had consumed enough liquor to knock him off his square. He reached for the girl who had entered the club with him and pulled her up into the DJ's booth. "Now everybody grab your lady and grab a glass of champagne so we can count it down," he said.

"Ten, nine, eight, seven, six, five, four, three, two, one—happy New Year!" Twin poured Cristal into his mouth straight from the bottle and then kissed his girl sloppily on the lips. "Now let's keep this shit going," he yelled into the microphone.

Everybody resumed their party antics . . . everyone except for Free and Big Lou. They watched Twin closely. He leaned into the girl's ear and said, "Go collect my money and take it to the back." Twin didn't realize that he still had the microphone in his hand. Everyone was too busy to notice the comment, but Free picked up on it.

"Go toward the bathroom and wait for the bitch to come back there," Free instructed. Big Lou nodded and made his way to the back of the club. Free's eyes watched intently as the girl went to the door. She was handed a backpack full of money. She then made her way to the bar and collected from there as well. *This nigga getting paid from the bar too!* Free thought to himself as dollar signs filled his eyes.

He looked up toward the VIP where Twin had the crowd captivated as he threw dollar bills into the air, making it rain on the crowd. He was flashing his cash. It was obvious that Twin wanted everybody to know he was paid.

Yeah, I see you, nigga, Free thought to himself.

He refocused his attention on the girl who was collecting Twin's money. He let her step a couple feet in front of him so that it would not be obvious that he was tailing her, and then he discreetly followed her down the dark, narrow hallway. When they were halfway down the hall, Free looked back to make sure the coast was clear and then pulled his .45 from his waist and grabbed the girl from behind. He put his hand over her mouth and pulled her into an empty office where Big Lou was already waiting.

"Listen . . . I'm not trying to hurt you. Don't scream; if you do, you ain't gon' leave me no choice. I'm just here for the money. Do you understand?" Free asked in a low voice as he whispered in her ear.

The girl nodded her head, and Free removed his hand from her mouth.

"Give me the money," Big Lou said as he roughly snatched the backpack away from her.

"Y'all niggas must really have a death wish," she said as she shook her head from side to side. She sucked her teeth and shifted her weight to one leg.

"What?" Free asked.

"You really think you about to make it out of this club with that cash? You must not know how Twin got his nickname. That nigga keep the twin desert eagles on him. You mu'fuckas ain't gon' make it three feet out this door before he put them to use."

Free grinned at the girl's attitude.

"You think yo' nigga big shit, huh? He's a pussy. I'll put something hot in his ass. Don't think ya' boy the only one with heat," Free threatened.

"Man, don't listen to this bitch. That nigga is drunk. He won't know what hit him until it's too late," Big Lou stated. They prepared to open the door to leave.

"All right, take your asses out there and get popped if you want to. He got four niggas watching each door with the pistols already locked and loaded. Twin ain't stupid. He knew somebody was gon' try to flex tonight. He is waiting to twist a nigga cap back. Ain't nobody walking out of here with them backpacks tonight. How does it feel to be fucked?"

"Stop flapping yo' dick, suckers," Big Lou stated as he chuckled at his own joke.

"Okay . . . go ahead. Go for what you know, but you ain't getting out of here tonight, at least not walking with that backpack in your hands. I take it that was your only reason for coming. So tell me, how does it feel to be fucked?"

Big Lou got heated and pushed the girl against the wall. He pointed his pistol in her face and said, "Look, you smart mouth bitch!"

Free was sure that Big Lou would put fear in the girl's heart. His six feet four inch frame and 280 pounds intimidated most people, but to his surprise, the girl didn't flinch.

"No, you look, nigga. The way I see it, you got one of two choices. You can either get laid out in this mu'fucka and get carried out in bags, or you can put me on, give me a cut, and I'll carry that bag out for you."

Big Lou released her neck and looked at Free, who was contemplating the situation.

"You Twin's bitch. You were just parading around here on his arm. Why would you help us? How I know you ain't setting us up?" Free asked suspiciously.

"A *bitch* like money," she replied, enunciating the word bitch to let him know she didn't appreciate being called out of her name.

"Fuck it. What you got in mind?"

Big Lou walked out of the room and walked directly up the VIP area. "Hold up. You ain't got a pass, so you can't get in," a bouncer said as he noticed that Big Lou wasn't wearing a VIP tag. Big Lou immediately got loud, causing a scene.

"Man, fuck all that! I paid money just like the rest of these niggas. Why I can't get in there? That's where the party at."

"You ain't got a tag, so you ain't getting in!" the bouncer said more forcefully this time. Big Lou threw a punch that knocked the bouncer out cold. He pulled his gun and started waving it in the air wildly. He fired a single shot into the air, causing pandemonium to erupt throughout the club. It was the perfect distraction. Then he ducked low as he bobbed and weaved, maneuvering his way through the crowd of bodies toward the front door.

"That's our cue," the girl said as she heard the screams inside the club. She ran out the back door. One of Twin's guards stopped her on her way out. "Yo', ma, where you going? You straight? You got Twin's money?"

"Yeah, I got it. Hurry up, get in there, somebody's shooting. You got to get Twin out of there," she said in a panicked voice as she put the backpack on her back.

"Wait outside while we clear this shit out," the bouncer replied as he pulled his gun and made his way into the club. She ran to her car and popped her trunk as she hurriedly placed the backpack inside.

"What you doing, ma? Give me the bag," Free said eagerly as he looked from left to right.

"Nigga, you ain't gon' get ghost on me. I'll meet you at Junior's tomorrow at noon. I'll bring the money with me; we'll split it up then. Now go before Twin sees you."

"Don't fuck with me, shorty," Free stated in a hushed tone as he grabbed her arm tightly.

"Look, I said I got you. Now go!"

Free reluctantly ran toward his car.

"Where the dough?" Big Lou asked as soon as Free got in.

"The bitch got it," Free replied. "She gon' meet me tomorrow, and we gon' split it up then."

"How you know she gon' show up?"

Free looked out his window as he watched Twin run out to the girl. She instantly began to cry and her act was so realistic that he had to let out a laugh. "She'll show."

The next day Free waited anxiously in the back of the restaurant as he watched the girl approach. She was wearing an all-white Versace sundress, and her hair was pulled back off her face in a loose ponytail. The side of her face was swollen, and her lip was busted. She carried the backpack at her side as she limped toward him.

Pain was written all over her face with each step that she took.

"Here's the money," she said.

"What happened to your face?" Free asked her as he wat-ched her sit down tenderly, trying to avoid causing herself any further pain.

"I took an ass-whooping for forty grand," she replied nonchalantly as if it were no big deal.

Free couldn't help but to laugh at the girl before him. She was unlike any chick that he had ever encountered. He was intrigued by her arrogant swagger, and her beauty was comparable to none.

"Let's go, shorty," he said as he stood up and took the backpack from her hands.

"Go where? I got to get my cut so I can get back before Twin notices I'm gone," she said.

"Fuck that nigga," Free said as he stood up and stared down at her. "You rolling with me."

"Excuse you? How you know I'm trying to fuck with you like that?" the girl replied with much attitude as she placed her hands on her hips.

"Don't front, ma. You wouldn't have let me get out of that club with your boy's cash if you weren't feeling a nigga."

A smile involuntarily graced her lips as she put her Dior sunglasses on her face to hide her true feelings. "I don't even know you," she replied sweetly, keeping up her hard exterior and playing hard to get.

"I'm Free," he replied as he held out his hand and turned to leave. "What's your name, ma?"

"Six," she hesitantly replied as she placed her hand in his and shook her head in doubt.

"Now you know me," Free said as he led her to his car.

"This is crazy," she told herself as she reluctantly followed behind him. "Twin will come after me."

"Listen, shorty, I'm not gon' let nobody harm you. All you got to do is keep it real with me. If you hold me down, I'll hold you down, a'ight?"

"Yeah, a'ight," Six replied with a seductive smile. "But can we leave town?"

Free stopped walking and looked Six directly in her eyes. "This nigga got you shook?"

"No, it's not that. I just want us to start fresh. A new city, a new beginning."

"Okay . . . but my man Big Lou coming with us." He wrapped his arm around her shoulders and then playfully pulled her to the car. It didn't matter that he didn't know Six from the next chick on the street. Free was a spontaneous person and blew wherever the wind took him. He chased the money, and as he walked toward his car, he chuckled thinking that he may have just met his match. "Where to?" he asked as he started his car.

"The Midwest," she replied. "I've got a father in Detroit. I haven't seen him since my mom died a few years ago."

When Free pulled away from the curb that day they became partners. Partners in crime, partners in life, partners in love. Everything was fifty-fifty with them. It was the beginning of the end.

Free opened his eyes when he felt the plane touch down in Detroit. He smiled as he reflected on the first time he had met Six. Just thinking about her made him love her more. As a man he felt like he was getting ready to give up a part of himself by marrying Six. Although he loved her more than life, and he planned to be with her, there was something about putting a ring on her finger that scared him. He had been planning this for some time now. For seven years he had been on his grind, trying to stack his chips so that he would be able to provide for himself and his woman. Six was spoiled. She had been ever since he met her. Free had stolen her from Twin, who had never spared her of any material possession. Free wanted to be able to give her more than any other man ever could. He wanted to give her the world, and he was ready to make her his wife. There was no questioning the fact that Six loved Free more than anything. She had been loyal to him from the time she laid eyes on him. He couldn't see his life without her, and it was time to make their relationship permanent.

Free stood slowly and followed Big Lou off the aircraft. They made their way through the corridors of the airport as they walked toward the baggage-pickup area.

"Yo', man, you serious about giving this shit up?" Big Lou asked. Big Lou and Free had been pulling capers together since they were young and coming up in Brooklyn. They had quickly made a name for themselves in New York, but after they had robbed Twin, they both skipped town and relocated to Detroit. They tried to stay low-key once they arrived in the Midwest, but they soon discovered that their new city was wide open and prime for the taking. They quickly returned to their old ways, and they reverted to the lifestyle that they knew best. Big Lou and Free were willing to get money by any means necessary as long as the amount of money outweighed the risk.

"Yeah, I'm done. This was my last hit. I've been stacking my paper for a minute now. Me and Six can kick back and just live, you know?" Free said.

"Yo', I don't know anything about that. I ain't gon' never leave this game alone," Big Lou replied.

"I hear you, fam," Free replied as they slapped hands and embraced briefly. "I'ma get at you."

Free and Big Lou grabbed their luggage and went their separate ways. Free located his silver Lexus Coupe and headed home. His hands were moist, and his heart felt as if it would beat out of his chest. Just the thought of settling down made his stomach turn. By marrying Six, he was committing himself to her for life. He was nervous, and he was pushing ninety-five miles per hour on the freeway trying to get to Six. He knew that she would be surprised. He wasn't due back in Detroit for another couple days, but he decided to finish up early and fly back to propose to her. *Is this the chick that I'm supposed to spend the rest of my life with? Is she really down for a nigga, like I'm down for her? Will I be the type of man that she needs me to be?* He knew that the answer to all of his questions was yes. Six was the woman for him. They completed each other, and the closer they became, the more intense his feelings for her became. The potency of his love for her even surprised him. She was his rib, and without her, he couldn't breathe.

As he pulled his luxury vehicle onto his street, he was so nervous that it felt like everything was moving in slow motion. He could see her candy-red, baby-mama Benz gleaming as it sat perfectly in their driveway. *Good, she's here,* he thought as his Lexus slid next to the curb in front of his house.

He reached inside of his jacket pocket and pulled out the box that held the ring inside. He opened it and stared at the flawless cut of the diamond. *It's all or nothing,* he thought as he snapped the box closed and exited the vehicle. He went to the front door, walking slowly as he thought back on his life as a single man. He had always been with Six, but he had enjoyed many chicks on the side over the years.

Damn, it's time to give all that up. It's time to fly straight, he thought to himself. Free reached inside his jean pockets in search of his house keys. "Damn, where those mu'fuckas at?" he muttered in frustration as he patted his pockets. He went back to his car to see if he had left the keys inside. He looked everywhere, but his hunt was fruitless.

He jogged back up to the house and rang the doorbell. He could hear the sound of R. Kelly's "12 Play" crooning throughout the house. The music was drowning out the sound of the doorbell as he continued to ring, waiting for Six to answer.

He grew impatient and made his way around the back of the house. He lifted his hand and banged on the back door, knocking hard so Six could hear him. To his surprise, the door cracked slightly. The smell of incense greeted him as soon as he stepped inside the door. All of the curtains were pulled closed, and the only light came from candles that had been strategically placed throughout the house.

"Six!" he yelled as he made his way through the house. He gripped the ring tightly as he rushed to find her. "Baby girl, where you at?" Free received no answer as he walked through the living room. The room was so dark that he lost his balance as he tripped over something that lay in the middle of the floor.

"Damn," he muttered as he reached to the wall and flicked the light switch. His eyes immediately focused on the odd pair of Tims that sat in the middle of his floor. *Fuck, this bitch done had a nigga in my house.*

Free's thoughts went from loving Six to being enraged with her in less than three seconds. He darted up the steps that led to his bedroom and heard moans coming from inside his room. He was squeezing the ring box so tightly that his knuckles hurt from the pressure. He walked to the bedroom door, and his suspicions were confirmed by the sight that he saw. His heart caught in his throat as he watched the love of his life blatantly betraying him. Her moans drowned his eardrums as another man grinded in and out of her, while her eyes rolled in the back of her head.

Free didn't know what happened next. He couldn't control his emotions. All rational thought went out of the window. Red and black filled his vision.

"Bitch, you fucking this nigga? You love this mu'fucka?"

Free was so hurt that darkness clouded his vision.

"You fucking this nigga?" he asked in utter distress as he pulled his pistol from his waistline.

Pow, pow, pow!

"Bitch, you fucking this nigga?"

Nothing but darkness and the sounds of the bullets entering flesh could be heard.

Pow, pow, pow!

So much red . . . blood flowed freely from the bodies of both victims. Blood on Free's hands . . . blood on his shirt, his shoes, blood in his eyes. The sound of his heart breaking fell on deaf ears. No one was alive to hear him.

Pow!

One final bullet . . . .

Pow!

Three Weeks Later

A pulsating pain shot through Six's body as she slowly opened her eyes. The room was dark, and she was unaware of her surroundings. *Beep, beep, beep, beep.* The steady tone of the machines around her was all that could be heard. The small sound seemed so loud inside her head. Each beep made a sharp explosion go off inside her brain, causing her great pain. Her eyes darted wildly around the room as she searched for something familiar. *Where am I? What happened?* she thought frantically as she tried to move her body. Her lungs felt deprived of air as she struggled to breathe deeply. She wanted to sit up, she wanted to scream for help, but her body would not co-operate. No matter how hard she tried, she was unable to move. Her throat felt like it was on fire, and her heart rate increased dramatically as fear gripped her body. *Beep, beep, beep, beep.* The sound of the machines intensified, and she heard the sound of people rushing into her room.

"Is she all right? What's happening to her?" Six heard Big Lou's voice, and her eyes scanned the many faces that were surrounding her bed as she tried to locate him.

"I'm sorry, sir, you have to wait outside. You can see her once we've stabilized her."

"Is she okay? Just tell me what's happening!" she heard Big Lou demand, his voice frantic with worry.

"Free!" she cried out. His voice was the only voice that she didn't hear. He was the one that she needed right now. *Where is he?*

"I need her calm. Her body is in shock," one of the doctors instructed. Six watched as a young nurse filled a syringe with fluid and injected it into her arm.

"No! Free—I want to see Free!" Six cried in a raspy tone. Her voice was almost inaudible. Her body was weak, but she still fought against the hospital staff as she begged to see her man.

"Look at my hand and count down with me," a doctor stated.

"Five, four, three, two . . ." Before he even got to *one* Six felt her eyelids close involuntarily, taking her to a temporary sanctuary of peace.

***

Six opened her eyes and immediately sensed the figure who was sitting in the chair beside her bed. She couldn't move her head to see who it was, but she could feel him watching her.

"Free," she whispered, her voice cracking.

"Free's not here, Six. It's me, Big Lou," he whispered as he stood up so that she could see him. "You had me worried for a minute, sis."

"Where is Free? What happened to me? I feel like I can't breathe. Why isn't he here?" she asked.

"You don't remember anything? You don't remember what happened?" Big Lou asked her in bewilderment.

"No, where is he, Lou?"

Before Big Lou could respond, a middle-aged black man entered the room. He was wearing a long lab coat with blue scrubs underneath. Big Lou was grateful for the interruption. He didn't know how to tell Six that Free was dead.

"Six Jones," the doctor stated as he walked up to her bed. He took off his stethoscope and placed the cold metal to her chest. "You are a very lucky young woman."

"What happened to me?" she asked the doctor. The doctor's face immediately expressed confusion as he looked toward Big Lou.

"She doesn't remember," Big Lou answered the doctor's question before he could even ask it.

"Well, Ms. Jones . . ." the doctor started. He was hesitant to inform her of her condition. "You were shot in the head. You are extremely lucky to be alive. That's why you are having such a hard time moving and breathing. During the shooting, a part of your brain called the cerebellum was injured. A part of the brain stem that controls your breathing was also injured. The massive head trauma that you have sustained has caused you to become immobile."

"I'm paralyzed?" Six whispered with tears in her eyes. She stared up toward the ceiling as she tried to process what the doctor was telling her.

"Not exactly. The damage is not permanent. But your body has to learn how to function again. That's why you are hooked up to the breathing machine. Your brain is not sending the correct signals to the rest of your body. You can't breathe or move on your own yet."

"Where is Free? I need him," she said as her tears began to flow. She gasped for air, struggling to breathe.

"She doesn't know?" the doctor asked as he looked toward Big Lou again.

"I can't tell her, yo'," Big Lou said as he gripped Six's hand and tears began to well in his own eyes.

"Tell me what?" she asked. "Where is he? Big Lou, where is Free?"

The doctor excused himself so that he could give them some privacy.

"Six, he's gone. He shot you; then he turned the gun on himself."

Six didn't respond. She stared at Big Lou as tears streamed endlessly down her face. *He can't be gone. He told me he would never leave me. Why would he do this to me? Free, I need you.* Her body shuddered as she thought about the death of Free. He had been her best friend and her heart. She couldn't find any words to describe how she felt; her heart was numb.

She closed her eyes, and images of Free entered her mind. The entire scene instantly came back to her as she played it back in her head. She could hear the blast from the gun in her ears. She could feel his pain as he asked her repeatedly, *Do you love this nigga? Do you love this nigga?* Six saw the spark from the barrel of the gun as Free pulled the trigger. "Oh my God! Big Lou! Oh God! He can't be gone. I can't do this without him. I need him," she cried. Tears of despair stained her cheeks as she lay helplessly in the hospital bed. "How did this happen? Where is he? Big Lou—"

"He's gone, Six . . . he's gone," Big Lou said as he held her hand.

"I just want to be alone," she stated as she closed her eyes.

Big Lou nodded slowly. "All right. I'll be right outside if you need me."

"Big Lou . . . when is his funeral?" Six asked before he stepped out.

"You've been in a coma for the past three weeks. The funeral was two weeks ago." He waited for her to reply, but when she didn't, he walked out of the room.

She couldn't stop the tears from escaping from her eyes. She was deeply hurt by Free's death. Her soul ached unbearably as she tried to imagine her life without him in it. *How did we get here? How did I let this happen?* Six stared at the ceiling as she thought about when her life began to spiral out of control.

Chapter One

One Year Earlier

Six stood beside the Audi S8 and tapped her foot anxiously as she waited for Free to exit the prison gates.

"You nervous?" Big Lou asked. She had been silent the entire trip there, and she seemed to be lost in her own thoughts. She silently hoped that her man would be the same as he was before he went in. She knew that the life and times of an inmate were hard and hoped that time hadn't changed him too much.

"Nah, I'm cool," she replied. Just as the words came from her mouth, the clanging of the large metal gates could be heard and Free came waltzing out. He turned around and stuck his middle fingers up at the guards who were positioned in the towers above each gate and then held his arms open for Six, who was running toward him full speed.

"Oh my God, baby, I missed you so much," she cried as she jumped into his arms and wrapped her arms tightly around his neck. He spun her around wildly and lifted her off the ground.

"Let me look at you," he said eagerly as he placed her on her feet and held up her hand as he twirled her around.

Six blushed as she felt Free's eyes roam her body. Big Lou approached the couple and embraced his friend.

"Big Lou!" Free exclaimed as he hugged his closest friend.

"Nigga, I see they were feeding your ass in there," Big Lou clowned as he noticed Free's change in appearance. Free had gained thirty or so pounds of muscle from eating the prison food and the everyday weight-lifting routine he had picked up while in prison.

"Shut up, Lou, my baby look good," Six defended playfully as she walked ahead of them to the car. When she was out of ear's reach Free turned to Big Lou.

"Yo', man how she been acting while I was away?" Free asked out of concern. He wanted to know what had been going on with her for the past three years. He had not expected her to wait for him and was pleasantly surprised that she had.

"Man, Six is the same chick she was when you left. She held you down. I never heard about her entertaining no other niggas. As far as I know, she was faithful. I know she been kind of hurting financially though. I been helping out when I can, but shit has changed, and times are rough, feel me?"

Free slapped hands with Big Lou and replied, "Yeah, I feel you. Thanks for watching out for her."

Beep, beep!

"Let's get out of here, baby," Six yelled from the car as she honked the horn lightly.

When Free got into the car Six pulled a shopping bag from the backseat. "Go ahead and get fresh, baby. That jail suit got to go."

Six drove home while Free and Big Lou let the road lull them to sleep. She looked over at her man who was sitting in the passenger seat and a tear fell from her eyes. She was so happy that he was finally home with her. The past three years had been one constant struggle. Emotionally and financially she was spent. The lawyers for Free's trial had taken most of their money, and she had been struggling to make her ends meet and maintain her high-class lifestyle. Things had gotten so bad that she had even began working as a bartender in a local strip joint called the Kitty

Kat. She knew that Free wouldn't like it, but she did what she had to do to maintain. They pulled up to her one-bedroom apartment, and she announced, "We're here, wake up."

Free drowsily looked up at the worn apartment building and then over at Six. "How long you been staying here?"

"About two years now," she replied. "I couldn't afford the condo," she stated, referring to the luxury high-rise condominium that she and Free had shared before his arrest.

Six exited the car, and Free looked toward the backseat and said, "Big Lou, I'll be right back. Let me get her settled." He got out of the car and put his hand on the small of Six's back as he followed her up to her apartment.

"What are we going to do?" Six asked Free. She was dead broke, and now that Free was home, she needed him to take care of her like he had always done.

"We gon' get money like we always have. You don't have to worry about anything, Six. I'm home now," he said as he caressed her hair.

"I know, but you don't know how hard it's been for me. I'm living in this fucking hellhole. I am struggling to pay the rent, and my bills are piled up to the ceiling!"

"What happened to the money we had stacked up before I went in?" Free asked.

"Your lawyers are what happened, Free," Six replied.

"How much we got left?"

"We ain't got shit left. It's about two thousand dollars in my account," Six whined.

"Two stacks! You blew through a hundred Gs in three years?" Free questioned.

"Why are you yelling at me? I told you your lawyers were expensive."

"I'm not yelling at you, ma. I'm just trying to understand why you hurting so bad. You ain't working? You couldn't get a gig?"

Six crossed her arms and replied, "Of course I got a job, Free. I wasn't just sitting back spending your dough. I'm working at the strip club, but that only goes so far."

Free's eyes widened in disapproval. "The club? You been shaking your ass for dollars while I've been locked up, showing all these niggas what belong to me?" he asked angrily.

"I'm bartending, Free, so calm down! What else was I supposed to do? I needed money, so Sparkle hooked me up with the bartending thing. Don't make it a bigger deal than what it is," Six defended, her voice raised a bit out of frustration.

"Damn, Six! I just got out of the joint today, and you already in my ear about some cash. Let me get my head together first. I never knew you to be the type to gold dig."

"Gold dig?" Six exclaimed. Her hands shot to her hips, and she scrunched her face in confusion. "Free, whatever! Your ass has been behind bars for the past three years, and not once have I thought of stepping out on you. I had the opportunity to say *fuck you* and move on to the next nigga, but I didn't. Yeah, I'm trying to find out what's up on some money. I'm broke. Niggas is knocking down my door asking for the rent . . . The world didn't stop when you went away. I still had to survive out here on my own."

Free turned his back to her and headed toward the door.

"Where are you going?" she yelled.

"To the block," he replied shortly. He was obviously steamed and wanted to get out of Six's presence before the small argument escalated. That's how they were . . . hot and cold . . . on and off . . . love and hate . . . their relationship wasn't one that had been pulled out of the pages of a fairy tale, but at the end of the day, all they had was one another. Despite the petty fights their love ran deep.

"You just got home. Your boys on the block are more important than me?"

Here she goes with that shit, Free thought to himself. Without answering, he left the house to clear his head. He was well aware that he needed to get on his grind. He still had an unsettled debt to pay, but the last thing he needed was Six stressing him out more by bitching over cash that he didn't have. He knew that she was high maintenance, but she would have to be patient until he came up with a hustle plan that would make him rich but wouldn't send him back to prison.

"You good?" Big Lou asked as Free got back into the car.

"Yeah, I'm good," he replied as he pulled away from the curb.

The liberated feeling that Free felt as he maneuvered his way through the city streets was better than anything that he had felt in a long time. The subwoofers in the car were on point as the two men pulled up onto Big Lou's block.

Big Lou and Free exited the vehicle to approach Big Lou's house. A familiar face called out to Lou.

"Big Lou! Hold up a minute, man," a voice yelled from up the street.

Free noticed a familiar face jog up the block toward them. Ronnie was the local weed man in Detroit. He got his supply from Big Lou, who had a crazy weed connect out of New York.

"Look at this mu'fucka," Big Lou whispered to Free. Ronnie's pants hung below his waist, and it was obvious that he was still wearing yesterday's drawers. The dingy color of the supposed-to-be white fabric and the dirt underneath his fingernails symbolized exactly how dirty the nigga was. His yellow gap-toothed smile and balled-up Force Ones were a dead giveaway to his grimy tactics. He kept looking behind him and from side to side as he approached. "This bum-ass nigga," Big Lou mumbled as he shifted his stance. "What up, Ronnie?"

"Yo', Big Lou, I need to holla at you about something, man," Ronnie replied as he continued to look from side to side.

"What up, fam? Time is money, nigga—talk," Big Lou stated.

Ronnie eyed Free suspiciously and then said, "Can we step inside or something? This a private matter, you know?"

"Nigga, you know Free. What's good?"

"No disrespect, Free. I just need to holla at Big Lou on some private shit, you know. I mean, I heard about your beef with them Russians, and

I'm not trying to be associated in that shit, you feel me?"

Free looked at Ronnie with a calm expression on his face and stated, "I don't know what you talking about. Handle your business though, bruh."

"Nigga, get the fuck out of here with all that privacy bullshit. Get at me when you ready to talk," Big Lou stated harshly as he and Free stepped up the sidewalk and sat down on the porch.

"What is up with your people?" Free asked as he made himself comfortable on Big Lou's porch, positioning himself so that he could see the entire length of the city block.

"Man, I ain't want to be all in your business, but word is out about you and that Russian cat. Niggas gon' be scared to fuck with you for a while. Word is you owe that mu'fucka like a mill or something."

"Niggas talk too much about shit they don't know, nah, mean," Free stated with apparent anger in his voice.

"What really happened? What did you do that got those Russians gunning for your head?"

"You remember the day I got locked up?" Free asked.

"Yeah, you was driving up to New York, but got pulled over by a cop. I never understood why you took them mu'fuckas on a high-speed chase. You was playing with them pigs," Big Lou stated with laughter in his voice. "Those crackers chased your ass all the way up Interstate 75."

"I didn't have a choice. I had fifteen keys in the car with me," Free admitted. He had never told anyone the true story of what had happened that day.

"And you only did three years? Free, you snitching?" Big Lou asked, knowing that the excessive amount of cocaine that Free had was enough to have gotten him a life sentence.

"Hell, nah. Come on, fam, you know me better than that. They ain't catch me with the bricks, just the pistol I had. I shook the police so I could get rid of the product. I tossed that shit. That type of weight would've put me under the jail. I didn't have a choice."

"What does all this have to do with the Russians?"

"It was their weight. Claude is out of a hundred and fifty thousand dollars."

"Damn! A hundred fifty?" Big Lou asked in disbelief.

"A hundred fifty," Free confirmed. "I just got out, and I know he's waiting to hear from me. I got to have something to offer when I call him, though. He gon' be trying to speak money, and that's something I don't have right now. Six is stressing over money, and I got this shit on my mind."

"Yo', you know I got you, fam. Whatever you need . . . well, not whatever, nigga. I ain't got a hundred fifty, but whatever else you need, I'm with you."

"Good looking out," Free said. "What I really need to know is how much the bricks going for?"

Free sat back on his best friend's porch and watched as Big Lou's block made money. Free could tell that a lot had changed since his reign had ended. The entire operation looked sloppy. Whoever was running things hadn't trained his people well enough. *These niggas is making transactions on street corners, and they keeping the work on 'em. Don't nobody stand on corners no more,* Free thought, disgusted at how off their hustle was.

"This cat named Brick got the joints for twenty-five a pop."

"Damn, a quarter a key," Free replied in disbelief. He had never paid more than 16.5 per kilo, and he didn't intend on starting now. He came to the conclusion that Brick was definitely overcharging. "He's taxing niggas like that?"

"Man, Brick the only one in the city that got 'em. There was a drought on the streets after you got hit. You know them Russians weren't fucking with none of us, so nobody could get their hands on work. Brick came through a couple months into your bid and took over. He had them for sale, and even though his shit ain't as good as the Russians, it was all we had to choose from. He knows he's the only one in town with the weight so he charges whatever he wants." Big Lou sat back in the white porch chair and smiled at Free. "You trying to get back on?"

Free shook his head and replied, "Hell, no, you know I ain't working underneath nobody, and I'm not paying no outrageous prices for the work either. I'll find another connect."

"Well, you might have a hard time getting anything off in Detroit. That nigga Britain is nutty as hell. If you ain't down with him, you ain't eating. He got all these niggas around here shook. The only niggas that's really getting money like that is Brick and his people. He's spoon-feeding everybody else."

"Fuck Brick. Ain't no man gon' stop me from eating, nah. mean?" Free asked as he thought about how badly he needed to come up. Just as the words came out his mouth, a caravan of expensive cars came rolling down Big Lou's block. Benzes,

Lexuses, and Escalades rolled slowly down the street. Loud music was coming out of the custom speakers of each vehicle, and each car was sitting on its own set of twenty-two inch rims. The windows of the cars were rolled up, and the faces of the men that sat inside were hidden by the dark tint.

"What is that all about?" Free inquired, nodding in the direction of the cars.

"That's Brick's young goon squad. Those are the only people that he keeps close to him. They ride around once a day to make their presence known."

Free knew that they were trying to stunt. They were riding high, and they wanted everybody in the city to know it. Once again, Free shook his head. Brick was running a drug ring that was destined to get him and his crew put in a federal prison. They had two qualities that were bound to get you locked up. They were flashy and stupid. Niggas riding around in one-hundred-thousand-dollar cars did nothing but draw attention to the already hot block where hustlers stood on corners alternating crack sales. *A couple years back, I would have stuck those flashy niggas up,* he thought to himself.

"You fucking with him?" Free asked.

Big Lou stood up and opened the screen door to the house. "Hell, nah. That drug shit is dead right now. A nigga like me values his freedom. You ain't seen the news?"

Free shook his head and then got up to follow Big Lou into the house.

"This shit has been all over the TV for weeks now. Brick got into some shit. One of his workers got nabbed a couple months ago. Dumb mu'fucka gon' try to venture out and do some side hustling. The nigga ended up selling to an undercover narc."

"Damn," Free commented.

"You ain't heard the most of it . . . Watch this shit," Big Lou said as he turned on his forty-inch plasma. CNNs Nancy Grace appeared on the screen, and her voice filled the room.

"According to federal prosecutor Brant Stall-worth, the government has a witness that can give in-depth testimonies regarding Britain Adams's involvement in an international drug ring. Britain Adams has a street alias of 'Brick,' and he has a loyal following of young men who have terrorized the city of Detroit. Allegedly, since his position as kingpin three years ago, the violent crime rate has skyrocketed in the area. He is charged with several counts of murder, distribution of a controlled substance, and extortion.

If convicted, Britain Adams will be facing a life sentence in a federal penitentiary."

Big Lou turned off the television and shook his head in contempt. "The worst part about it is that the key witness is one of the cats he kept in his inner circle, so he knows everything. I'm talking names of the connect, stash spots, where bodies lie . . . the whole nine."

"Sound like your man Brick don't know who's who in his own camp," Free stated. *This nigga Brick set himself up. You always supposed to know who you got in your circle,* he thought.

"Word on the street is he got a fed in his pocket that can tell him where they holding the witness. Only thing is he can't do anything about it. They got the scope on him tough. The nigga can't take a shit without the feds knowing about it."

"Sound like his days are numbered," Free said as he shook his head from side to side.

"Looks that way, don't it?" Big Lou agreed.

For the first time Free realized that the drug game was dried up. The clientele was there, but Brick had made it too hot for anybody to do anything. He looked at Big Lou and then said, "I'ma get at you later, fam."

They slapped hands, and Free prepared to leave. Before he walked out of the door, Big Lou called out to him.

"Yo', Free!"

Free stopped walking and turned to face his friend.

"Let me know if you need me."

"Thanks, man, I'ma get at you."

Nighttime had fallen quickly, and Free was mentally exhausted from trying to come up with some type of plan. He was riding through the city streets when he noticed the flashing red and blue lights behind him. He pulled over to the side of the road and placed his hands on the steering wheel. He didn't want to give the cop any reason to jump stupid, so he waited patiently as he approached the window.

"Alfree Woodard," the officer announced smugly. Free already knew who it was. He recognized his voice. It was the same detective who had locked him up three years ago. He had some type of personal vendetta against Free.

"Detective Wade," Free acknowledged as he nodded, still keeping his hands on the wheel. He knew that Wade wouldn't have a problem putting a bullet in him, so he made sure that he didn't make the wrong move.

"It's kind of late for you to be out here, ain't it?"

"Just running to the store for my girl," Free replied. The detective laughed slightly and repeated, "Running to the store for your girl." His demeanor turned hostile as he continued. "Cut the bullshit, Free. I'm watching you. I'm here waiting for the opportunity to send you back to prison." With those words Detective Lonnie Wade walked back to his unmarked squad car and drove off, winking at Free before he was out of sight.

"Fuck!" Free yelled out as he hit the dashboard. He knew that the detective's eyes would be on him for awhile. If he made any type of attempt to reenter the drug game, the detective would send him back to prison, and this time it would be for the long haul. *How am I going to come up with this money?*

Six felt guilty about the argument that she had started with Free. She knew that he was a good man. He had always treated her with respect and showered her with material possessions. *Damn, I shouldn't have gone off like I did. I know if he's got it, I've got it. I got to stick by his side right now and let him know that I'm here.*

Six was consumed by her thoughts as she prepared a romantic atmosphere for her man to come home to. She was so used to him spoiling her, and now that he couldn't, she was upset. She knew that she was going to have to let Free know that she was there through whatever. He had carried her for so long and only stopped because he had been arrested. She knew that it was her turn to be strong for her man, and that is exactly what she planned to do from that point on. She looked at the clock that read 4:30 A.M. and felt her heart sink. She didn't even know if Free planned to come home. The empty knot in the bottom of her stomach had her sick with uncertainty. He had never stayed out all night before, but they both had said things that should have never been spoken, and she knew that he was feeling the exact same way that she was . . . guilty. She lit every candle in the house and turned out the lights, creating a romantic ambiance in the tiny apartment. Then she showered and slipped into a black Victoria's Secret camisole and matching thong. Turning on the song that she and Free fell asleep to every night, Six sat back and listened as Biggie kicked his lyrics to "Me & My Bitch."

But you was my bitch, the one who'd never snitch

Love me when I'm broke or when I'm filthy fuckin' rich

Six's eyes watched the clock and as each minute passed a little bit of her heart broke even more. Free was her best friend, and she needed him to know that she was down for him. She knew that Free wasn't the type of man who would be down for long. He would pick up the broken pieces; she would just have to give him time. She was stressed and had blown up out of frustration, but in the back of her mind, she knew that he would take care of her. She balled up on the couch and stared at the front door. *I hope he comes home.*

As if her thoughts had summoned him the locks clicked on the front door, and Free walked in. He stared at Six as she lay on the couch, and she returned his gaze. They both could sense the other's remorse, but they didn't feel that it was necessary to speak any words. They knew each other like the backs of their own hand and already knew what the other was thinking.

He sighed and walked over to her, he lifted her head and sat down. She rested her head in his lap as he stroked her hair and inhaled the scent of her love spell body spray. His touch was so gentle that he sent shivers up her spine. Six was so glad that Free had come home. Everything that she had planned on saying was easily forgotten. She just felt good being in his presence.

"I'm sorry," she whispered. "I understand what you're going through, baby, and I am here for you. We're together for life, and when you are down, I am here to help pick you up. You take care of me, Free; you always have, and I know you always will. I was just aggravated with everything. It was hard for me while you were away. I put pressure on you when it wasn't necessary. I love you, Free, and I'm here with you. I know it's only a matter of time before we're on top again, but I want you to know that I'm with you even when we're on the bottom."

Free sat back and listened as Six talked. He knew the type of chick who he had on his team. Free understood why Six was worried, but he was a man, and he was going to make their ends meet by any means necessary. She was his queen, and he had spoiled her so much that she had become accustomed to living the life. He was determined to provide her with that lifestyle again. He knew that until he could do that she would stick by his side.

Looking down at Six as her head rested in his lap, all of his tensions melted away. Just being near her again felt good. Everything about the two of them was always so right . . . so on point as if their existence had been synchronized to the same clock. He looked at her voluptuous figure and felt the swell of his dick rise against his jeans.

Six sat up and straddled Free, grinding her hips against his concealed manhood. She kissed him seductively, exploring his mouth with her tongue. Her body moved to the rhythm of the song, and Free's hands gripped her ample behind, his fingertips leaving dents in her soft skin as her breasts pressed against his chest. Free grabbed Six's backside firmly and looked down at the thong that had disappeared between the crack of her ass. He picked her up with her legs still wrapped around him and carried her into the bedroom.

Her fat lips were a beautiful sight to Free. He had gone his entire stretch in prison without feeling the inside of a woman, and her engorged clitoris made his mouth water in anticipation. He licked his lips as he placed a finger to Six's opening. She sucked his long finger inside of her, using her vaginal muscles to entice her man.

Free closed his eyes as he felt her walls tighten around his finger. Six was soaked in her own juices, and she couldn't wait for her man to please her. She held onto him tightly as he gently placed her on the bed and pulled off the tiny thong. Six sat up, reached for his belt buckle, and removed Free's jeans. His thick eight inches stood at attention in her face, and she couldn't help but to taste him. She devoured him into her mouth, making him disappear and reappear over and over. Free placed his hands on her head and gently guided her as she sucked him like a lollipop, her tongue stroking the vein on the back of his shaft.

Six's head game was superb and it was designed just for him. Her full lips, deep throat, and slick tongue were all trained personally by Free, and all she wanted to do was please him. She ran her tongue up and down his length and kissed the tip gently, causing his toes to curl.

Free pushed Six back onto the bed, and they positioned themselves into the sixty-nine position. He opened her lips with his tongue and tasted her wetness as he gently ravaged her womanly pearl. His tongue flicked back and forth, fast and then slow . . . firm and then soft.

"Aggh," she moaned as she rotated her hips, making love to Free's mouth. The better he made her feel, the better she sucked his dick. She couldn't help it, he was making her go crazy, and she wanted to please him until he exploded. She wanted him to release all of the built-up tension from years of lockup.

Moans couldn't help but to escape her lips as he tickled her insides with his fingers and caressed her clit with his tongue. She was riding his face like a cowboy and moving her head up and down like she was bobbing for apples. Free was large, and she wanted him inside of her, but she was feeling too good to stop him. He ate her out, and she hit him off until they both reached their climax. She swallowed his seed leaving his manhood spotless, and her back arched with the grace of a ballerina as she came in his mouth. They both had reached ecstasy and in the process released all of their built-up anxiety.

Makeup sex was the best between Six and Free. It was so good that sometimes they looked forward to fighting just so they could make up all over again. Too exhausted to get up and do anything, Six wrapped herself in Free's arms.

"I'ma take care of you. You deserve the best, and that's what I'm gon' give you. That's my word."

"I already have the best. The world is ours, Free."

Free had to smile at her words because he knew that she was the perfect woman for him and that she would always hold him down.

"The world is ours, ma."

With those words, they drifted into a comfortable sleep.

Chapter Two

It seemed like the morning came too quickly because Six was still groggy and exhausted from the night before. She felt the covers being lifted off her and frowned as the draft of cold morning air caused goose bumps to form on her skin. She knew that Free wanted to pick up where they had left off, but she was too tired.

"Baby stop . . ." she mumbled as she felt him run his finger down her thigh. "Free, your hands are cold . . . stop," she whined as she kept her eyes closed, not wanting to awaken fully. It wasn't until she heard the shower running did Six realize something wasn't right. The sound of running water sparked confusion in her mind.

"Six! Bring me some soap out of the closet!" she heard Free yell. The hands that were touching her body suddenly felt like tiny knives scratching her skin as she realized that they didn't belong to Free. She sat up instantly to find three white men standing in the room, one of whom was standing over her tracing the outline of her ass with a black .38.

"Fre—" Six tried to yell out to Free, but before she could even get his name out of her mouth, a sweaty hand covered it, silencing her, and three pistols were aimed in her direction, the .38-caliber pistol pointed directly at her temple.

"Shut up, bitch," one of them calmly instructed.

Six's heart felt like it had sunk into her stomach, and fear filled her body. In any other situation she would have known how to react. She would have taken her chances and reached for the nightstand where her .22 pistol was kept. She would have warned Free that someone was in the house. She would have done something, but this situation was different. She had been caught off guard, and the man that had the steel pressed to the side of her head intimidated her. There was something about the way that he looked at her that told her he wouldn't hesitate to pull the trigger. For the first time in a long time she was afraid. She didn't know what was going to happen or even why they had come.

The men's eyes ogled her body, and she wanted to pull up the covers, but was frozen in place. Everyone in the room heard the running water stop. The men cocked their weapons, and Six's body stiffened when she heard the hammer to the

.38-caliber pistol pull back. Six did the only thing that she could do and lifted her eyes to the sky and prayed silently. *Please God, don't let them kill Free . . . please don't let him come into this room.* Six wasn't even worried about her well-being; The only thing that she could think of was Free. She didn't know what she would do if something happened to him.

Free wrapped a towel around his waist and then made his way into the bedroom. He opened the door and the sight of a gun threatening Six's existence enraged him. He ran toward the bed, but was halted by a tall white man who aimed a .357 Ruger in his direction.

"Free!" Six yelled out, afraid that he would be shot. Her heart was beating like a drum and tears began to swell in her eyes.

Free's mind was focused on getting to her; he wasn't thinking about the hole that the Ruger would leave through his chest if fired. He grabbed the wrist of the man and punched him hard in the face causing blood to flood from his nose.

"Aghh, fuck!" He man yelled out in pain as he cupped his face with both hands and dropped to his knees in excruciation. In one swift movement, Free snatched the weapon from his hands and pointed it toward the bed where the infamous

Claude Jean, member of the Russian mafia, stood next to a terrified Six. Free was working straight off of emotion and didn't notice the third Russian intruder until he had his gun pressed against Six's head. Claude laughed as he jabbed his gun into her skin.

"Free, what the fuck are you doing? What are you, Superman now?" He continued to chuckle and then firmly stated, "Don't be stupid. Put the gun down." Free hesitated as he looked at Six, who had closed her eyes.

"What are you going to do?" Claude continued, "Are you going to kill me, Free? Before you even pull the trigger, her brains will be all over the bedspread." Free dropped the gun and glared at Claude, who now had the gun on Six's bare breasts, the cold steel making her dark nipples stand at attention and enraging Free even more. Free could see Six trembling, and his jaw clenched as he gritted his teeth.

"What is a woman so beautiful doing with a man like Free?" Claude asked as he continued to fondle Six's nipples with the gun. She slapped his hand away, and he chuckled. "Someone like you could be living lavishly. If you play your cards right, I might make you my mistress," Claude said as he lusted after Six's naked frame. He pulled back the covers so that he could see her entire body.

"Don't touch me," Six spoke through clenched teeth in a frightened tone as she roughly snatched the covers to cover herself.

"You black bitches have no manners. Your men don't know how to train you. I was trying to offer you something more than Free could ever give you, but your eyes tell me you have chosen Free. So fuck it. You're his whore, so his debt just became your debt too."

Free was infuriated at the disrespect, but he knew that Claude would not hesitate to kill Six, so he kept his cool.

"She must be the reason why you forgot to contact me and let me know you were released from prison."

"If you touch her—"

"Yeah, yeah, yeah . . . Let's skip the dramatics, Free. You know how I work. If I wanted to kill the bitch, she'd already be dead. I came here to talk about my money."

Free remained silent and stared at Six as she stared frightfully back at him.

"You take fifteen kilos of my good, pure, Russian cocaine on consignment, and then you get busted with them. That's $150,000 worth of product I'm out of. Then you get out of prison and don't even contact me to make arrangements. That bothers me, Free. . . . I shouldn't have to come here looking for you."

"I've only been out a couple hours, Claude. I'll have the money. . . . You know I'm good for it," Free stated defiantly, the apparent anger showing in his voice.

"You used to be good for it! That's the only reason why you are still breathing. You served your time like a man, and not once did you mention my family's name. I respect you for that, but I won't commend you for it. That is what you were supposed to do. We want our money, Free. $150,000 plus interest."

"How much?" Free asked.

"$250,000 . . . a quarter million. You have six months. If you don't come up with my money by then, I will murder everybody that you have ever loved, beginning with her."

The Russians walked out of the room, but before Claude exited the apartment he yelled out, "I will be back in six months."

As soon as they heard the door close, Free rushed to Six's side as she broke down in his arms. She buried her head in his shoulders, and her body shook uncontrollably as Free rocked back and forth trying to console her. It was the first time that he had ever seen Six so weak, and it hurt him deeply. He didn't say anything, he just held onto her. He loved her more than he loved himself, and he was determined to keep her safe. He would not let Claude touch her again . . . Free would be prepared next time, and the consequences would be death.

"Shh, it's all right. . . . You're safe now," Free comforted her.

"What are we gonna do, Free?" Six asked as the tears flowed down her face. Six was afraid, not only for herself but for Free. She couldn't live without him by her side, and she was afraid of what was going to happen next.

"Don't worry about none of this. I'm gon' handle it," Free said reassuringly as a thousand thoughts raced through his mind.

"Let's just leave. . . . We can leave Detroit tonight," Six pleaded. She could see the look on Free's face, and she knew that running from the Russians was not an option. "Free, please. Let's just pick up and go. . . . We can go as far away from here as we can. They will never find us. Just say you'll leave with me."

As much as Free wanted to give Six her way, he couldn't, not in this circumstance. "Nah, I owe them those bricks. I'm a man, and I'm gonna pay my debt, but for them touching you, they gon' die. That's my word." Free watched as Six nodded her head. He felt guilty about dragging her into his business with the Russians. It had nothing to do with her, but he knew that she was his weakness. The Russians would use her against him, and he was determined to get her out of it.

For the rest of the day, Six and Free stayed away from each other. They were both consumed by their own thoughts. Free knew that his situation was crucial. He needed money like he needed air in his lungs, and if he didn't come up with a resolution soon, the Russians would shatter his world. Not only did he need to grind to please Six, he needed to grind to save her life. He knew that Claude would make good on his threat, and Free would die before he let anything happen to her.

Six had so much on her mind she couldn't think straight. Free was in trouble, and no matter how much he tried to downplay the situation, she knew that it was serious. It was a matter of life and death. Six sat in the middle of their bed with her legs crossed and the monthly bills sitting in front of her. It seemed like her life had been turned upside down, and the only thing that could fix her problems was money. Rent was due tomorrow, and they didn't have enough to cover everything. Six didn't know what to do. She knew that Free's mind was occupied with thoughts of Claude, and she didn't want to bother him with anything else.

It was crazy how quickly her life had changed. Before Free had been sent to prison, she had everything she could ever want, and there were never any arguments or worries over funds. Now that was all that seemed to matter. How they were going to pay off their debts? Whether it was Claude, bill collectors, or the landlord . . . they all wanted their money. Six got up and walked into the living room where Free was sitting in deep contemplation.

"I'ma hit the block for a minute," he said as he stood and wrapped his arms around Six's waist.

"Okay," she replied absentmindedly. She knew that he was going to handle some business. She had some business to tend to of her own, and this would give her the opportunity to take care of it. "I think I might go see my dad," Six said, knowing that he would help her with the bills and be able to calm her soul about the money issues.

Six's father had been helping her cover her rent since Free had first gone to jail. No matter how long or hard she worked, her pockets always came up short, and she always had to go to her daddy to help pay the extra. Ben Jones didn't mind, though. Free had helped him out plenty of times before he went in for his three-year stretch. Free always made sure Jones's pockets were right, and he always took good care of his only daughter, so Jones felt obligated to return the favor. Six was close to her father. Before Free, he was the only person who ever cared about her, and she knew that he would always help her if he could. She knocked on his door lightly and waited anxiously for him to answer.

"Hey, Daddy," she said when he opened the door. She tried to put on her best smile and sound as normal as possible, but her father knew her too well. He could see right through her.

"Hey, baby girl," he greeted as he opened the door for her and led her inside. Her father lived in a small house in a modest neighborhood on the outskirts of the city. "I hear Free's out."

"Yeah, he's home. Three years is a long time. I'm just glad that we're together again," Six explained with worried eyes.

Jones sensed his daughter's disposition and asked, "If you're so happy, why are you sitting here all frowned up, looking like you are carrying the weight of the world on your shoulders?"

Six shrugged her shoulders and responded, "Things are just real tight right now, Daddy. You know I was barely making it while Free was locked up. I guess I never thought about what we would do when he got out. I just assumed that things would go back to how they were before." Six watched as her daddy pulled out a bag of weed and rolled up a joint. He was an OG and gave the best advice when he was high.

"Six, part of the reason why I gave Free my blessing regarding you is because I knew that he would do anything to give you the world. I knew that he would take care of you, and he has. He just finished doing a bid, so it's gon' take him a minute to get back on his feet. Until then, you have to hold him down. You know that I'm gon' help you in any way that I can, and Free don't have to know about that. He's a real man, and you belong to him now. He ain't gon' want no other man taking care of his home. . . . It don't matter that I'm your daddy. So this can be our secret."

Jones reached in his pocket and handed Six two thousand dollars, enough to pay her rent, and then continued. "I know Free had quite a bit of change saved up, but he paid that price for his freedom. Those damn lawyers will do that to you. The important thing is that he's out. You don't know what it's like being a young black man with a record, baby girl. Your daddy knows about that, so I can relate to what Free is going through. Don't sweat him. . . . Just ride with him. Let him get used to breathing this free air again. Once he gets used to being home, everything will fall into place." He stopped talking to puff on the joint while Six sat in his old La-Z-Boy, absorbing her father's words.

"Is that all that's bothering you?" Jones asked his daughter, noticing her contemplation.

Six nodded her head and replied, "Yeah, Daddy, that's it. I'm good; I just got a lot on my mind." Six had decided on the way there not to tell her father about their run-in with the Russians. She didn't want him worrying, and she also didn't want her father confronting the Russians. She knew that he didn't care how big or dangerous Claude's operation was—her father would kill them or die in the process for laying hands on his little girl. In his day, he was a notorious murder for hire and would put in work if he had to. *No, it's better if I keep that to myself,* she thought as she rose from her seat and hugged her father.

"I love you, Daddy. Thanks for everything."

"I love you too, baby girl," he said in between tokes. "Tell Free to come see me. He's been out for a couple days now, and he ain't come to holla at your old man. I need to talk to him about something."

"I will," Six replied as she walked toward the door.

"Six!" Jones called out.

"Yeah, Daddy?" she said as she turned around to face him.

"Word on the street is Free owes the Russians a lot of money. You need to be careful," he warned her.

"You know how niggas talk in the streets, Daddy. Everybody spreading rumors. Free is good," Six replied quickly. She didn't realize that he already knew about Free's beef with the Russians. For him to know about it meant that it was traveling down the hood grapevine and she knew that couldn't be a good thing.

"Yeah, I hear you holding your man down, not wanting to put his business out. I already know the deal so there ain't no need to lie to me. Those Russian mu'fuckas ain't nothing to play with."

"I hear you, Daddy."

"I'm serious, Six. Be careful. The best way to get to a man is through his woman. Always remember that. Do you still have the pistol I bought you for your eighteenth birthday?"

Six lifted her pants leg and revealed the tiny .22 pistol that was strapped to her ankle in a holster.

"That's my girl. Make sure Free comes to see me and soon."

He kissed Six on her forehead and she walked out the door. Just as she stepped off of his porch she saw a pearl-white Rolls-Royce pull up in front of her father's house. *Who is driving a Royce through the hood?* She asked herself as she made her way to her car. A dark-skinned dude with a five o'clock shadow stepped out of the vehicle. He was clean in a white linen button-down and matching baggy linen shorts. Six silently wondered what the guy was doing there to see her father. She could feel his eyes watching her from behind the designer shades he wore and she turned her head to avoid his gaze as she passed him. He nodded a hello at her as he stepped to the side to watch her walk by, but she disregarded him without acknowledgement. She was too busy thinking about her father's warning regarding the Russians.

Her father's words kept playing in her head and Six was grateful for his wisdom. He was always there when she needed him and he always made her feel better when she had a problem. The simple fact that he had warned her about the Russians told her that they were dangerous and made her think about their intrusion that morning. *If we can pay off the Russians, everything will be okay.*

Six began plotting ways for them to come up. She knew that they needed a hustle, she just didn't know what it would be. It was clear that Free couldn't enter the dope game. There was too big of a risk associated with it. Free would need to move some serious weight in order to achieve that goal. *The dope game is out. I can't see my baby get locked up again, so we definitely not fucking with that. We're in this together. I know Free is gon' try to carry this by himself, but I'm not taking no for an answer. We have to get this money.*

Notes

ORDER FORM
URBAN BOOKS, LLC
78 E. Industry Ct
Deer Park, NY 11729

Name: (please print):_____

Address:_____

City/State:_____

Zip:_____

QTY	TITLES	PRICE
	16 On The Block	14.95
	A Girl From Flint	14.95
	A Pimp's Life	14.95
	Baltimore Chronicles	14.95
	Baltimore Chronicles 2	14.95
	Betrayal	14.95
	Black Diamond	14.95

Shipping and handling-add $3.50 for 1st book, then $1.75 for each additional book.
Please send a check payable to:
Urban Books, LLC
Please allow 4-6 weeks for delivery

ORDER FORM
URBAN BOOKS, LLC
78 E. Industry Ct
Deer Park, NY 11729

Name: (please print):_____

Address:_____

City/State:_____

Zip:_____

QTY	TITLES	PRICE
	Black Diamond 2	14.95
	Black Friday	14.95
	Both Sides Of The Fence	14.95
	Both Sides Of The Fence 2	14.95
	California Connection	14.95
	California Connection 2	14.95

Shipping and handling-add $3.50 for 1st book, then $1.75 for each additional book.

Please send a check payable to:

Urban Books, LLC

Please allow 4-6 weeks for delivery

ORDER FORM
URBAN BOOKS, LLC
78 E. Industry Ct
Deer Park, NY 11729

Name: (please print):_____

Address:_____

City/State:_____

Zip:_____

QTY	TITLES	PRICE
	Cheesecake And Teardrops	14.95
	Congratulations	14.95
	Crazy In Love	14.95
	Cyber Case	14.95
	Denim Diaries	14.95
	Diary Of A Mad First Lady	14.95
	Diary Of A Stalker	14.95

Shipping and handling-add $3.50 for 1st book, then $1.75 for each additional book.
Please send a check payable to:
Urban Books, LLC
Please allow 4-6 weeks for delivery

ORDER FORM
URBAN BOOKS, LLC
78 E. Industry Ct
Deer Park, NY 11729

Name: (please print):_____

Address:_____

City/State:_____

Zip:_____

QTY	TITLES	PRICE
	Hush	14.95
	If It Isn't love	14.95
	Kiss Kiss Bang Bang	14.95
	Last Breath	14.95
	Little Black Girl Lost	14.95
	Little Black Girl Lost 2	14.95

Shipping and handling-add $3.50 for 1st book, then $1.75 for each additional book.
Please send a check payable to:
Urban Books, LLC
Please allow 4-6 weeks for delivery

ORDER FORM
URBAN BOOKS, LLC
78 E. Industry Ct
Deer Park, NY 11729

Name: (please print):_____

Address:_____

City/State:_____

Zip:_____

QTY	TITLES	PRICE

Shipping and handling-add $3.50 for 1st book, then $1.75 for each additional book.
Please send a check payable to:
Urban Books, LLC
Please allow 4-6 weeks for delivery